Hollow Land

J.E. Byrne

J.E.Byrne

www.authorjebyrne.com

ISBN-13: 978-1503104068

Hollow Land

Cover photo courtesy of Gabby Cressman

and Lexi Colgan.

Sabol Communications, LLC

www.sabolcommunications.com

J.E.Byrne

DEDICATION

To my mother Elizabeth,

for always guiding me toward The Mountain.

J.E.Byrne

If a man owns a hundred sheep,

and one of them wanders away,

will he not leave the ninety-nine on the hills

and go to look for the one that wandered off?

Matthew 18:12

J.E.Byrne

CONTENTS

J.E.Byrne

From *Dead Land*, Chapter 26 "Wisdom Falls"

The next day we awoke to silent skies. Since the rain had stopped, we prepared ourselves for our continued quest. I could see David, Lance, and Josh poring over the Eirmanns' map. I walked over to join in the discussion. The map showed that Mount Elbert was in the middle of Colorado, straightforward from where we probably were in Ohio. All we had to do was move forward and we would eventually run smack into it. It couldn't have been made any easier for us. Maybe God was in our midst; even I, the rationalist, was beginning to believe a little bit. Ruth walked over and peered at the map. She gave me a smile.

"Seems like our destination has been mapped out for us by an omnipotent surveyor," she said.

"I was just considering the same idea," I replied.

Ruth and I walked back to our sleeping bags and began to pack.

"How are you holding up?" she asked.

"I'm okay, how are you?"

"Fine," she replied. "Are you feeling any better?"

"Yeah, thanks." Poor Ruth had been forced to witness my many symptoms of poor health the past couple of months. She looked like she was going to say something else when Lance came over. He softly took my hands and kissed my cheek.

"Time to move out," he said. He helped me gather my things, and then assisted both Ruth and Leah in assembling theirs. He was a bit old-fashioned, but chivalry can be kind of a turn-on. When the thirteen of us were ready, off we ventured. Mt. Elbert, here we come.

We walked all day before David signaled us to stop. I was exhausted. I had cramps on top of cramps. After a debriefing, we all decided it was time to probe into the wilderness to find our camping place. Lance and David walked in front to protect us from any unseen dangers. I was looking forward to getting some sleep. Although I had been feeling much better the past few weeks, I still tired easily. As we stepped over fallen leaves and branches, I felt a pulling in my lower abdomen. I pressed my hand over it to relieve the pain.

"You okay?" asked Ruth.

"Yeah," I replied, "Just my usual aches and pains. I'm rather getting used to them." I attempted to joke off the concerns I probably should have been having.

"Sarah, when we make camp will you sit by me? I would like to speak with you about something."

"Sure." I had to admit I was curious what she wanted to discuss; it was going to be hard to wait.

After forty-five minutes or so, we stopped to make camp. Ruth and I laid out our sleeping bags near where Jack was beginning to gather scraps of wood for a small fire. Leah quickly set up her bag next to Ruth. Everyone else randomly unpacked all they had left in the world and gladly lay down their weary bodies. The Eirmanns had blankets collected from their car that they laid down like a king-sized bed for their brood; I really hoped they would make it. A dangerous and probably barren Colorado mountain seemed like an unlikely destination for a group of post-apocalyptic survivors; but we all seemed convinced that it was real. As I was beginning to get lost in my thoughts, Ruth touched me gently. She motioned for me to follow her. I guess our talk demanded some privacy. We walked until we were out of the group's earshot. Ruth motioned for me to sit down. I sat with some light discomfort, but readily perked for our conversation.

"Sarah, I have wanted to talk with you for some time," she said.

"Okay," I replied with a bit of trepidation, while I adjusted myself on a bed of dead leaves.

"Sarah, do you remember when you found me?"

"Yes."

"Well," she continued, "I had just been through a pregnancy. I had observed and felt nine months of carrying my child." Ruth looked down when she said the words 'my child.' This was painful to her; why did she want to bring this up?

"Yes, I remember," I replied.

"Sarah, I have been watching you. I see in you, that is, I recognize...Sarah, I don't know how else to say this—you're pregnant."

The world stopped for the second time. Pregnant? Me? Now? I felt like I was in one of those movies where everything turns silent and moves in black and white slow motion; and then suddenly, *snap*, all becomes loud, fast, clear, and in color.

"What? No! What makes you think that?"

"Sarah, is it possible that you are pregnant? I mean, did you..."

I cut her off. "No! I mean, well, there is a chance." How could I ever explain this to her? How could I admit to her how I was violated? I thought I would never have to speak of it again. I thought I had buried it deep with Jenna.

"Ruth?" I looked into her eyes and I saw the truth. It all made sense. The small bit of blood months ago, then no period since. The sore breasts, the swollen belly, the fatigue. I thought I had cancer; but no, I was pregnant. I was pregnant with one of those animals' child. I was so sickened with the news that I leaned over and threw up the remaining green bile in my stomach.

"I am pregnant," I said aloud as I looked back at Ruth.

"You're pregnant?" David was standing over us. His confused eyes met mine.

"Oh my God, oh my God," I cried out as I ran off into the woods. I needed to be alone. I ran and ran as fast as I could until I stumbled upon a tree limb or something. I fell onto my side. I just lay there, unwilling to move. I could hear David calling my name. I didn't want him to find me. Not ever.

"Leave me alone, please!" I waited. He called my name again and again. He said he needed to talk with me. He said he was not going to give up. I waited and let him yell until his voice went hoarse. Finally, I heard Ruth come and coax him away.

"I'll be back later, Sarah. I need to see you," he called out. How could I let him know that I never intended to face him again?

Alone in the woods, my panic set in. What was I going to do? How could I keep going, knowing that a child was growing inside of me? I must be like, almost four months pregnant; in another couple of months, it would be hard for me to keep up with the others. If I could even go full term, in five months' time I would give birth, and then what would I do? Would they leave me behind? Would they care for me like I did for Ruth? Would I want them to? I was scared. I wanted to die.

"God, if you really do exist, why are you doing this to me? Why have you left me here with so much to bear? I am so weak; I can't possibly handle this. Please do not be so far from me, trouble is near and there is no one to help. I am afraid. God, can you hear me? Please, can you help me?" I

sat quietly and listened, but I could not hear anything. I felt
alone. I was alone. I began to cry. I cried myself to sleep.

"Sarah."

"Yes?"

"It's me, Lance. Are you okay?"

"No."

"What's wrong?"

"I'm pregnant."

"I know."

"What?" Did Ruth tell you?

"No."

"You knew? How?"

Lance sat next to me and used his arms to raise me
to a seated position.

"The first time I looked at you, I knew. You
glowed, you exhaled it. I couldn't take my eyes off of you."

I was dumbfounded. I looked deeply into his eyes.

"You mean, you are happy about this?" I asked.

"Yes," he said. "I think it's the only good thing in
this screwed-up, so-called dead land, and I have wanted to
take care of you and this baby from the first moment I saw
you."

He leaned toward me and ran his hand down my
cheek. I felt both relieved and numb. I leaned in closer to
him.

"Thank you," I said.

Lance softly brushed my lips with his. I was so
alone, so scared.

"I love you, Sarah."

I kissed him back. Oh, how I longed for love, for
affection. I was so lonely, so starving for attention. Lance
pressed his mouth upon mine. I opened my mouth for him
and let our kiss melt. I placed my hands under his layers of
shirts and felt his hard chest. It was soft, warm, and just

slightly hairy. I lowered my hands to his abdomen. It felt strong and rippled with muscle. He trembled with my touch; it made me feel powerful. I undid his belt. I unbuttoned his jeans. I placed my hand down there. It, too, was warm, strong, and hard. It made me feel important to be able to give him this much pleasure. I felt his hands under my many sweaters. He gently touched my stomach; he seemed to lovingly swirl his hands around my growing belly. Next his hands inched up to my swollen breasts. He lifted my clothes so he could look at my proof of pregnancy. Instead of feeling ugly, I felt beautiful. I saw through his eyes excitement and passion at my body, full with life. I allowed him to press against me, considered him entering me; it wasn't like he could get me pregnant or anything. Lance touched my breasts and began whispering in my ear. What was he saying?

"David's here."

"What?"

"David sees us."

Lance's voice seemed pleased in revealing this news, and he did not stop in his pursuit of my body. I was foggy in the moment and looked up. I saw David. He did come back, as he had promised. He looked stunned. I pushed Lance away.

"David!" I screamed.

"I'm sorry," he said, but he would not leave. "Sarah, I have been looking for you. I need to talk with you. I was scared before and…" I cut him off.

"Go away, David!" I yelled at him. "Get out of here!" He paused. He shook his head. I watched as he turned around and left. He left me again.

I sat up and covered myself. What would he think of me now? First, he finds out I'm pregnant; then, he sees me about to have sex with yet another man. I was such a disaster.

"Sarah, it's okay," Lance tried to say with comfort. "Don't worry about him. He just wanted to make sure you were safe, and he saw that you were. He can go back to his own life now and stop worrying about yours. I'll take care of you now."

But I love him, I wanted to say. *Come back and fight for me*, I wanted to scream! But I didn't say anything. Instead I just kept silent and dreaded everything. I pulled my sweater down, covering myself.

It was then that Lance poured out his plan to me. He proposed that he and I take off together, that we start a life together. We didn't need the others, he said. He would take care of me. He would find us a house away from the dangers of civilization. He would find us food. He would provide for me and care for me until I gave birth. He would protect me and my child. We would live as normal of a life as we could. He would love me and defend me.

I wanted that. I needed it.

"Okay," I said.

Lance and I decided that we would leave that evening while everyone was asleep. I couldn't face them. I could never face them again. I sent Lance back to camp. He was to explain to the group that I was fine, and that I just needed some privacy.

My whole life I have felt like an outsider, and here I was, alienated again. Just when I thought I had found another family, I isolated myself from them. I wanted people to like me, to trust me, but I was always messing things up. Why couldn't I just be normal, accepting of my flaws and the outreach of others? Why did I always have to be so hard, so full of pride? Damn it, I just hated myself sometimes. Thankfully, Lance didn't seem to care if I was a screw-up. I felt like I could be flawed with him; the others were just too perfect. I could never measure. I would never reach that mountain. It would always be out of my reach. But maybe it was enough, knowing that the others would make it.

I placed my hand into the front pocket of my backpack and pulled out the last old, stale piece of the chocolate bar from Jack and his dad's campfire. I had been secretly saving it for Jack. I smiled. I would miss him, but I knew he would be safe with David and the others. I would only be a burden to the rest of them now. I would slow their journey, one now invigorated with an exact destination. This time, I would be unselfish. I would stay behind so that they could make it. It was enough. I felt relief. I had made the right decision.

Lance came and got me when the others had gone to sleep. I quietly snuck over toward the fire's last embers. I saw David lying in between Jack and Jared. I just stood there and stared at his sleeping form. I wondered why he wasn't with Claire. I wondered if I should wake him. I wondered many things. I silently laid the wrapped chocolate next to Jack. I stole back and lay on my bag for a while. I needed to get some rest before my flight. I looked up into the dead sky. How I longed to see life. Then I remembered that life was in me. It was growing in me. I looked at Lance. It was time to go. So we did. We left. I didn't turn around to look back. It was too painful.

As I walked in the darkness, I could see. In the morning, they would awaken to find Lance and me gone. At first, there would be concern; maybe even panic. But within minutes, Jack would find my gift placed by his side. He would know from the gesture that I was okay, and that I left by choice. He would reassure the others. He would tell them that I would be back. Jack would never stop believing in me, and for that I remain eternally grateful.

I walked just behind Lance. Leah didn't leave with us; Lance convinced me that she was better off with Ruth. We walked briskly and silently so that the others would not hear us and pursue. I still had gnawing doubts in my decision to leave with Lance, but felt certainty in not wanting to be a burden to the others. I wanted them to make it, I really did. It didn't matter for Lance or for me; he did not believe, and I did not merit.

I figured it was August. It was good we were travelling south before a cold fall would arrive. I reached into my pocket for my iPhone to check the date. Old habits are hard to break. Like me, my cell was gone; I had given it away. It was okay; I was resigned to my circumstances. I got what I deserved. I swallowed hard and decided to pretend things were better than they were. As I followed my fated path, I walked with a symphony of lament on my imaginary iPod. It told me that there were certain things in life that I could not change. I wished that David could hear the music. Then he would know the helplessness I felt as I entered my time in the wilderness. I was the lost sheep. I wondered if he would ever come looking for me. I hoped not; in a strange way, I wanted to be lost. I wanted to be left alone. I wanted him to feel my absence. He chose Claire.

Lance kept motioning for me to hurry, but I felt sluggish. I tried to pick up the pace. I tripped over something and fell on my knees. I placed my hands on the ground to push myself back up. They touched something cold and stiff. It was a person. It was dead. I looked closely and let out a scream, because it was Leah.

1

Lost

    I quickly lifted myself up and onto my knees, crawling far away from the body. I didn't want to be so close to death. I could hear Lance, who had gotten far ahead of me, turning around and calling my name. I couldn't speak. I couldn't move. I couldn't do much of anything. Finally, shaken into action, I dug my right hand deeply into my pocket and pulled out my lighter. I flicked it on so that Lance could see me through the blinding darkness. I watched as he jogged over to where I had stationed myself, sitting on the damp and musty ground. I could tell that he was afraid for my safety. I let go of the igniter just before it burned my fingertips. He gently knelt down beside me before he spoke.

"Sarah," he whispered. "What's wrong? Are you okay? Is it the baby?"

"I'm fine," I answered. "It's not me; it's Leah." He looked at me, confused.

"Sarah," he continued, "Leah's not here. We left her behind with the others, remember?"

Lance must have thought I was having some kind of traumatic mental lapse. I looked directly into his eyes, as if it could soften the blow of truth. "Leah is dead," I said.

"How could you know that? Are you having another one of your dreams or visions?" he asked. "I thought we both agreed that they were not real, that they didn't mean anything."

Maybe he was right. Maybe it was just a vision. I carefully stood up and reignited my light. Slowly, I walked over to where I had originally tripped and fallen. I stuck my flame close to the ground, and there lying on her side, was a very dead Leah. Lance walked over and saw his sister's body. Seemingly frozen with disbelief, we both stared at her in the flickering light. Her eyes were open and alert as if she had an important message to share, even in death. I strained to hear the supernal voice I had come to know, but it remained eerily silent. I knelt down by her body. Upon closer inspection I could see that there was blood running down the side of Leah's face. Her skull above her right ear and across her temple was crushed. Leah didn't just die; someone had killed her. I quickly stood and backed away.

Her backpack was untouched; nothing was stolen. Lance alerted me to the danger.

"We've got to get out of here. We need to move now!" he whispered in my ear as he extinguished his lighter and took mine from my hand, snuffing its flame. He grabbed my arm and guided me away from Leah, and onward, stumbling through our obstacle course of ubiquitous darkness, leaves, sticks, and other woodland debris. He led me back to where he had left his makeshift wheelbarrow, the one that held his now invalid motorcycle engine, and then he used it to clear our path. We travelled quickly and efficiently, not stopping to talk or rest, for most of the night. Finally, when I knew that I could go no further, I reached out and touched his arm in an effort to signal our stop.

"Lance, I can't go any further. I need to rest."

I watched as he lit a candle and illuminated our path. All around us was endless landscape, teasing no signs of civilization. Lance guided me over to a large tree that stood, a solitary pillar in its dying backdrop. He helped me unload my pack, and then he laid my sleeping bag out underneath of the tree's shelter. We sat and leaned back against the enormous trunk. I figured the tree had to be at least three-hundred years old. As I rested against its foundation, I could feel its energy. I thought about all it must have seen in its hundreds of years, and the stories it could tell if only it could speak – ones of natives seeking shelter under its young leaves or of early settlers bravely travelling west with everything that they owned packed along with them. Accounts of young men killing and dying for land, country, or their version of truth; stories of progress and setbacks, one step forward and two steps back. And now, this three-hundred-year-old tree stood here witnessing its own demise, and with it, all of humanity's too.

I considered all that had happened in the past four months since the explosion that, while allowing me to live, stole from me my life. I closed my eyes to forget, but the action only heightened my vision of the incineration of everyone I knew; my friends, my family, all who had been safely tucked away at 3:10 in the morning. I saw the brutal attack of Derek and experienced the ensuing moments when I was raped by strangers who left me carrying a child. I felt tears forming in my eyes, and I closed them even tighter, forcing the lament to trickle down my face. Yet, the recent memories still came.

I saw myself hunched over Jack's father, Rick, as I forced CPR on his body, already choked from life by his diseased lungs trying to survive the poisoned air; I envisioned Jack's innocent face as he mourned his father, and the morning after when he revealed to me that we had shared the same dream of a mountain, far away to the west, promising refuge. I saw Ruth as she held out to me her dead infant Seth; Jenna as she took off on her very last adventure; David, dark and troubled in all of his suffering and the burden of leadership. My mind envisioned Lance and Leah and the promise of a working engine; the Eirmann's, weak and starving, waiting in the abandoned rest stop for someone to rescue them; and the darkness that surrounded us all. It felt like we, the survivors, had all been suddenly placed on the dark side of the moon with no way to ever return to the light.

No matter how hard I closed my eyes, I could not stop seeing. I felt Lance nudge me on the shoulder. He handed me a bottle of water. Even though I was incredibly thirsty, I just held it on my lap. I didn't really see a point in my baptism; why prolong my inevitable death? But just then, warmth began spreading throughout my chest and rose into my cheeks. I felt it flush down into my legs and even into my feet and toes. Finally, the teasing of life spread into my abdomen where I felt movement, I felt it. I mean I felt her. I knew that she was a girl. As if a butterfly was set loose in my stomach, I felt the new life inside of me. And then I raised the water to my lips and drank the elixir of life, because it was no longer just about me; it was about her. I had to stay alive for her.

I looked over at Lance. He was staring out into the darkness, trying to process all that had happened.

"Do you think she was following us?"

"Yes," he said as he turned and looked at me. For the first time, I could see stress on his face. In the light of the candle, his normally alert eyes looked tired and small lines had formed on his forehead.

"What do you think happened to her?"

"I don't know," he replied. But with his answer, he turned away from me.

And as I leaned back against my friend in truth, the tree, I closed my eyes. I breathed in deeply and with my exhale, acknowledged that I was lost in the wilderness with a man whom I didn't know at all. I had made a poor choice, and with it, had taken the wrong path. I was headed into the valley of the shadow of death.

2

Guns

I opened my eyes and again looked at Lance. He
was sitting still and staring ahead – looking at nothing. He
offered me no explanations or any false attempts of solace. I
could tell that he, too, didn't know what to do. I turned
away, gently sliding my hands from my face to my growing
abdomen. And then again I closed my eyes, this time in
hope of enlightenment. How did I cope with the difficult
things in life before this, before the earth gave up? I
delivered myself to my life before, three years ago, to the
day of my father's funeral. It was September. I remember
being so angry that the sun still rose even though the man
that I had loved more than anything was gone. How could
sunrises, sunsets, constellations, and gravity just 'go on'

when my world had ended? I opened my eyes with a start and peered into the present gloom. How could *I* go on, now that *everyone's* world had ended?

Again I retreated to my past. Back at the funeral, I saw my parents' friends, co-workers, and family members as they poured into the small church. I remember them trying to give me little smiles or waves, awkwardly avoiding any direct conversation. I felt relieved, knowing that I could avoid most of the lame sentiments I would have heard: "I'm so sorry for your loss," "I loved your dad too," or my ultimate favorite, "I know how you must feel." Really? Are you me? How could you possibly know how I feel? I was so angry. I sat in my cold and insufferably uncomfortable pew and pretended to listen to the minister. He was reciting some psalm, one which my mother had printed on the funeral cards. I looked down at the card in my hands. On the front was a picture of a blue sky with celestial white clouds and large, overbearing praying hands, and on the back were the words to the psalm. I remember trying to memorize its poetry in an attempt to distract myself from the intolerable service that I was being forced to endure. Somehow the words gave me comfort. Reading them passed the time, and before I knew it, Ben was nudging me that it was time to lead the procession out of the church. I wondered if I could still remember... "The Lord is my shepherd, I shall not want. Something about green pastures and still waters...restoration..." *and yes, I remembered this part clearly,* "even though I walk through the valley of the shadow of death, I will fear no evil, because you are with me."

I opened my eyes. I turned and looked at Lance. I startled him with my voice. "I'm going back."

He abruptly turned and looked at me. "You can't go back."

"Yes, I can," I said. I climbed up onto my knees and began packing my things. Lance leaned over and tried to touch me on the shoulders, but I backed away from him. I had made my decision. I was going back to find the others, to find David.

"Sarah," Lance said forcefully, "you can't go back. It's too dangerous. Look at what happened to Leah."

I stopped rolling up my bag and looked at him. "And what exactly happened to Leah?"

"She was killed Sarah! Somebody bashed her brains out. Do you want that to happen to you?"

"You know that's not what I'm asking," I said. "Why would someone kill Leah? What risk was she to anyone? She could barely hold a conversation let alone a threat. Her backpack was in-tact. Nothing was stolen. There was no motive other than that someone wanted her dead. Who killed her Lance?"

"I don't know Sarah," he said. "You've got to believe me; I don't know what happened to her. But I won't let the same thing happen to you."

"Why would it? Why would someone want to kill me? I'm weak, pregnant, and I have a backpack full of nothing. I am neither a threat nor a temptation to anyone."

"That's not true," he said. "You are a huge threat."

I turned and looked at him. Our voices had raised and we were standing face-to-face in the darkness.

"What does that mean?" I asked.

"Sarah," he began. But he never got to finish, because before any explanations or confessions spilled, gunshots rang out. I felt Lance's heavy body fall on top of mine as he forced me to the ground. Next I watched, dumbfounded, as he pulled a small gun out of his left sock, leaned upward and began shooting into the darkness in the direction of the gunfire. I tried to hold my ears while I coiled under the protection of Lance's body. The noise was deafening. Several more shots rang out before the air returned to its silence. Lance's body remained heavy on top of mine.

"Sarah, are you okay?"

"Yes. Where did you get the gun?"

"Does it matter?" he asked.

"Yes."

"I've always had it. I need to protect you." He continued, "It sounded like there were two of them, two different shooters."

"Are they dead?"

"I think so."

I felt the relief of safety. Lance had saved me. He gently rolled off of me and onto the ground. I quickly placed my hands on top of my coat. I had to check. My fingers came away sticky and warm. Panicked, I forced my hands underneath, under the coat, under my sweatshirt. My skin felt dry and firm. She was safe. I sighed with relief, and then turned to see Lance just as he was slinking to the ground. It was then that I realized that I was covered in his blood.

3

Steel

"Lance," I said as I crawled over to him. "My God, you're shot, you're bleeding."

"I'm okay," he answered.

But he didn't look okay. In the dim light of the still flickering candle I could see that his face had grown pale and that beads of sweat were forming along the top of his forehead.

"Where did it get you?"

"I'm not sure. Feels like my left shoulder."

I went to lift his heavy, woolen sweater to take a look at the wound when he grabbed my wrist to stop me.

"Sarah, we have to make sure they're both dead first."

"But Lance, you said they were, and besides you need help."

J.E.Byrne

"First, make sure they are *both* dead. Otherwise, there will be no hope for either of us." He leaned over and blew out the candle. Next, he opened my right hand and placed his small revolver inside of its palm. "Go find them. If either is still alive, shoot. Shoot to kill."

I looked down at my trembling hand. I had never before held a gun. The metal felt hard and cold in my hands, just like the sentence it was created to carry out.

"I don't know how," I said in a weak voice. I used my left hand to nervously tuck pieces of my long hair back into my hat.

Lance reached out and gently moved my right index finger onto the trigger. "It's just like in the movies," he said. "Point at the bad guys and pull the trigger. Now go, hurry. Sarah," he said as he covered my loaded hand in his, "you can do this. You're stronger than you think. Stay low and silent. Now go. Save us."

I slowly rose to my feet. Keeping my body low I followed my outstretched right arm. I felt that if it lead the way, I would somehow be safer. It was still so dark, so cold, so lifeless; I couldn't see anything except the shadows of empty trees. Relying on instinct, I took a few steps toward the place where I thought I had heard the shots originate. I stopped and listened intensely. I heard nothing except for the rapid pounding of my own heart. I took a few more steps, and still there was nothing. I followed this pattern until I was pretty sure I had reached the post of the strangers. I crouched down onto my ankles. I waited. I listened. It seemed like an eternity before I heard the single snap of a twig. It must have only been twenty yards to my left. I lifted my quivering right arm and pointed toward the sound. Another snap. I straightened my arm in essential confidence, held my breath, and then fired a single shot. It was loud and sent vibrations throughout the veins in my arm. I heard only the sound of gravity as the weight of a body slumped to the ground. My hand was trembling in its decision over someone else's life. I quickly dug my left hand into my coat pocket and felt around for my lighter. I pulled it out and flicked it on to see the status of my victim. As I walked closer, I could see in the dim flame the forms of two bodies. One was in the background, seemingly dead from Lance's original round. The other was forward five or so steps, still holding a gun inside of a slightly opened hand. I gently nudged the hand with my foot to be sure there was no life. The body was still. I had killed it. I knelt down and placed my hands on the body. It was still warm. I turned it over. I had not killed an *it*; I had killed a woman. Her dark brown hair was tangled and matted, and her face was covered in filth. I looked into her eyes. They were vacant as if the soul had left the body long before her death. Next I walked over to her partner. It was a man. He was big and hairy, maybe older than she. He, too, was covered in grimy dirt. They no longer looked human; they looked like animals. I wondered who they were. I wondered why they wanted us dead. *Us.* I remembered Lance. I needed to get back and check on his wound. I quickly surveyed our enemies. Lance said they were the bad guys. Did that make us the good ones? Who could tell anymore? Neither person was carrying a backpack or any travelling items with them for that matter. The woman had a pistol, the man a hunting rifle. Instinctively, I grabbed both.

"Lance," I called out as I ran back toward his resting place, disoriented in the adrenaline of the moment. "Lance!"

"Over here," he called back. His voice sounded weak and labored. I needed to hurry.

"They're dead," I coldly stated as if I had killed many times before.

"Good shot," he whispered.

I laid down the rifle and revolver, but secretly slipped the woman's small gun into my pocket.

Looking up, I could see that Lance had taken off his sweater and was pressing it firmly over his wound. It was on his upper left shoulder. I flicked on my lighter and had him hold the light steady with his right hand while I carefully lifted the makeshift bandage. Blood was still streaming out of the wound. I looked at his face. Lance was ashen and his lips were slightly blue. I was losing him.

I placed the sweater back over the wound and pressed hard. Lance grimaced and let the lighter fall to the ground. I sat back on my heels and tried to gather my thoughts. I opened my pack to get him some water. It was empty. I reached over and grabbed Lance's bag. It only held one half-filled bottle of water and an almost empty box of old cereal. I placed the water to his mouth and he drank. I knew that I would need more than this. I could not save him without any supplies. I couldn't save either of us. My mind began to race. *I could leave him. He probably won't make it anyway. This is my chance to get away. I have a gun. I know how to use it. I can protect myself. I can go back and find the others, find David. I am free.* And then again strange words came. It felt like they had formed somewhere deep inside of me and then were forced upward and into my psyche. I tried to push them away. I knew that I didn't want to obey their command. But they came anyway, just as they always did, "Truly I tell you, whatever you do for one of the least of these, you do for me." *But I'm not even sure who you are*, I thought. I looked down at Lance's face. His breathing was rapid, yet even. His eyes were closed as if he completely trusted his life to me. I sighed heavily. Maybe if I could save him, I could in some way save myself. I was injured too. I was wounded with the reality that I had killed another. I thought about the man and woman, how they were travelling with only guns and no supplies. How could they have survived without any provisions? Maybe they had food and medicine stashed somewhere. Maybe this section of the woods was their territory and they were tracking us. I lifted Lance's sweater. The bleeding had slowed, but it had not stopped. He was shivering. He opened his eyes and looked at me, pleading for life. *Damn it,* I thought, *I was going to do the right thing.* I lay both of our sleeping bags over him and gently touched his forehead.

"I'll be back," I promised. Then I lifted the covers and placed the dead man's hunting rifle under Lance's right arm. "In case any unwelcome visitors come by," I said.

I stuck my hand into my left pocket to feel the security of the small gun, and then grabbed my empty pack and threw it over my shoulder, carrying the other piece of steel in my right hand. Then I ran off toward the direction of our predators. I had to find their shelter and I had to find it fast.

J.E.Byrne

4

Blood

My feet kept twisting and turning in the small pockets of withered vegetation as I ran into the woods. I strained my eyes to make out the substantial shadows of trees and bushes. While I wanted to save Lance, I could not risk injuring myself or my child. I paused for a moment, ignited my lighter, and followed the path back to the bodies of our attackers. I figured their shelter couldn't be far behind. Occasionally, I would ignite my lighter and scan the area, then quickly turn it off, petrified that the killers were not alone. I listened for sounds of others, but heard only stillness, if that was a sound. There was no breeze, no rain, no crickets or birds or snapping twigs – only the soft steps from my own two feet. Eventually I came to a section of land filled with the shadows of several tall trees. Each was thin and bare, life swept off by the toxic environment. Lifting my flickering light, I looked up into their canopies,

34

straining my eyes, hoping to catch some sign of life. As I lowered my eyes down their large frames, I caught the shadow of a small structure. It looked like the remnant of a child's tree house or an old deer stand or some type of wildlife viewing area. Taking in the view of my skeletal surroundings, I surmised that these woods were probably once teemed with animals, but where were those creatures now? I knew that I didn't have time to ponder such things; I needed to find provisions. I needed water, food, and any type of medical supplies I could get my hands on. Lance and I had nothing; my only hope was that this shelter could provide something. Forcing myself out of my thoughts, I walked right up to the base of the shelter. I ran my lighter over the rickety planks of wood nailed to the tree. Carefully, I placed my gloved hands on the fourth rung and lifted my feet to the bottom one. I quickly climbed up and into the shelter. I realized that Lance and I had probably walked right by this fixture; the man and woman watching us, carefully plotting our deaths and ironically sealing theirs. Little did they know that we had nothing of value to offer them. Once in the shelter, I sat down and took a deep breath. The floor felt soft and damp beneath my legs. The wood moved slightly under my weight. The normally stale air held a pungent stench. It smelled almost like metal, like an old penny or something. I had witnessed this smell before, the night when I found Ruth, and recently when I had lifted the sweater off of Lance's wound. It was the smell of blood. I hesitantly raised my lighter and gave it a charge. I ran my eyes along the belly of the shelter noting its treasures. I quickly ripped two worn road maps off of the wall closest to me. The nails that had held them pulled out easily, taking with them small pieces of rotted wood. I grabbed a large flask resting on the floor to my left and gave it a shake. Thankfully it was not empty. Next to it were two cans of beans. I stuffed the flask and the cans into my backpack. As I continued scanning the shelter, I saw several blankets and towels thrown into the right corner of the shelter. I quickly began sorting through the pile, figuring that I could rip thin towels into strips, making bandages for Lance's wound. Most of the towels smelled like the dead landscape, so I carefully sifted through the pile until I found the remnants of one that was relatively clean. I stuffed it into my pack and continued through the pile, hoping for one or two more. As I lifted the remaining few, the rotten and metallic smell increased, overtaking me with nausea, and with the unveiling of the last blanket, I froze. Bones. Human bones. I fell back in shock. My breathing became rapid as I closed my eyes to the truth. These people were predators, and Lance and I were their prey.

"Oh God," I cried out as I quickly climbed out of the shelter, missing the bottom rungs and falling hard to the ground. "God!" I screamed as I looked upward. I wasn't sure he was listening so I yelled even louder. "God, don't you ever let me lose my humanity!" I pleaded with him. "Do you hear me God? No matter how bad it gets, how desperate I become, please don't ever let me lose my humanity!" And then I ran off to try and save Lance.

5

Identity

My eyes burned with tears and my heart with life as
I fumbled my way back to the area where I had left him.
I felt defeated. Life was meant to be lived, not taken.
Desperate to save Lance, I called out to him.

"Lance!" There was no immediate answer and I
feared I was too late. "Lance!" I yelled louder and with
a tinge of panic.

"Over here," I heard in a weak voice. I closed my
eyes, tightly squeezing out my tears and then breathed
deeply in relief as I ran toward his voice. As I
approached, I could see the silhouette of his frame
sitting up, leaning against the tree, still holding his
sweater protectively against his wound. The blankets
had fallen off of his upper body, yet he did not look
cold. I removed my glove and swiftly touched his
forehead. It was hot with fever. His normally confident

eyes looked scared as they searched mine for hope. I
gently moved his hand away and lifted his sweater to
peer at his wound. The bleeding still had not stopped. I
moved my other hand behind his shoulder in search of
an exit wound; there wasn't one. I felt his body quiver
at my touch. Realizing that the bullet had to be lodged
somewhere inside of his shoulder, I inspected its entry
point; encircled in red, it was swollen and giving off
heat.

"It has to come out," Lance said.

"How are we going to do that?" I asked.

"You're going to have to do it Sarah. It's my only
chance."

I looked into his eyes and nodded hesitantly. He
was right. I balled up his sweater and placed it back on
the bleeding wound. Lance winced as I applied pressure
– and then I lifted his right hand to hold it in place. I
thought about all that I had in my possession that could
possibly help us. Quickly, I dug my hands inside of my
backpack to empty its contents. It held the newly
acquired towel from the deer stand, the half-full flask,
the two road maps, the cans of beans, and some old
candles. I lit one of the candles, and then laid
everything out on top of our sleeping bags,
contemplating the inventory. Next, I reached into my
left sock and pulled out my butcher knife, the one I had
taken from Rick's kitchen all those days ago, back
when it first happened. Rick. Jack. David. Jenna. I
closed my eyes in the painful memories. Then I opened
them because I didn't have time to mourn my losses. I
had to try to prevent another. I opened the flask and
took a whiff. Smelled like whiskey, or scotch or
something like that; I could never tell the difference, but
it reminded me of watching old Civil War movies with

my dad. In the films, medics in make-shift hospital tents used whiskey as both anesthesia and antiseptic. I looked at Lance's wound. I was a medic in a makeshift hospital. I could do this. I had to. I put the flask to his lips and told him to swallow. He gulped down a large amount of the burning nepenthe, and then lay back onto the ground.

I ripped the towel into three strips and then poured a tiny bit of the flask's alcohol on my hands in an attempt to sanitize them. Next I lifted Lance's hand, taking it off the wound and laying it on the ground by his side. I looked deeply into his eyes, and he returned my gaze, both of us silently acknowledging how much pain I was about to inflict upon him. I picked up a small stick from the ground and held it in front of his mouth. Understanding, he opened his jaws, and clenched the stick between his teeth. I grabbed his right hand with my free left hand and held it firm. With my right hand, I poured a small amount of the alcohol onto his open wound. I watched as he bit down on the stick and felt him squeeze my left hand in agony. I placed my right index finger into the wound, inside of his body, deeper and deeper until I could feel the hardness of the bullet. It was lodged inside of his collar bone. I had to free it from its hold. I was going to need a better grip. Lance was going to need some more alcohol.

"I'm going to make a small cut so that I can reach in and grab the bullet."

He nodded. I held up the flask. I removed the stick between his jaws and poured another rich helping of anesthesia into his mouth as Lance leaned slightly forward. He swallowed eagerly and then lay back in resignation of what was to come. I placed the stick back into his mouth and placed his right arm under the

39

blanket so that he could not reach up and grab my hands during surgery. Next I ignited my lighter and ran its flame along the blade of my knife in the hope of killing at least some of the germs that I was sure littered its edge. I moved the candle, my surgical lamp, closer. Then I grabbed one of my make-shift bandages and placed it in my left hand, while holding the knife in my right. I watched as my hand trembled under its responsibility. I had to calm down.

"Please God," I said aloud as I watched my hand soften.

"Ready?" I asked him. His eyes were focused on mine.

Then he closed them tightly and nodded.

Please don't let me kill him, I thought.

Slowly I lowered the knife to his shoulder. I watched as its point pierced his skin. My hand, now surprisingly steady, allowed me to remain focused only on the size of the incision. With my left hand, I swabbed the blood that gushed from the newly opened wound. Occasionally, Lance flinched under my knife, yet he stoically accepted his fate and never cried out or reached for me to stop. When I was sure the opening was large enough, I inserted my two fingers and thumb into the hole and grabbed the bullet. I tugged and he suffered, but eventually I was able to release the culprit of his suffering. I dropped the hard piece of metal onto the sleeping bag and poured the remaining alcohol over the wound. Lance cried out in pain as he bit down on the piece of wood. Tears ran down my face as I wadded up the pieces of ripped towel and pushed them firmly on top of his bleeding wound. I held them there while I lay my head down on his chest sobbing in relief. I could feel the weight of his arm as he laid it on top of my back.

"Thank you," he said. And then he passed out.

After a few minutes, I slid out from under his hold and slowly arose, sitting back against the tree, with one hand still pressing down on his wound. I waited for the bleeding to stop; I hoped that it would stop. And after what felt like forever, it did. I changed the bandages and kept them pressed against his chest. His breathing was steady and his forehead felt cooler. Maybe I had saved him. It was too soon to be sure. I looked down at my operating room. In the candlelight, I could see the blood-covered bullet I had removed from Lance's shoulder, rags clotted with blood, my knife covered in blood…blood was everywhere. I leaned back and went to tuck free strands of my hair back into my hat with my trembling fingers, when I saw that they, too, were covered in blood. And as I stared at my crimson-stained hands, I felt the enormity of my actions. In an attempt to save us, I had killed another. In a moment of panic, I grabbed my water bottle to rinse my hands of the act, but the bottle was empty. I had no water. I had no way of getting the blood off of my hands. I began to panic. I frantically and futilely began rubbing my hands against my sleeping bag. They would not get clean. They could not get clean. My hands revealed me as the killer I had become, and that damned spot could never be cleaned. I blew out the candle, embracing my fate.

J.E.Byrne

6

Able

Exhausted, I lay down next to Lance, pulling the covers over us both. I allowed the consequences of emotion to consume me. No longer having to pretend that I was strong, I wept until tears would no longer come. Except for his labored breathing, Lance remained lifeless at my side. Drained of all energy and emotion, I fell into a troubled sleep. My dreams were a collage of my life. I saw myself jumping into the waves at the Jersey shore with Alex and Chelsea…pushing my little brother Ben on this bike, teaching him to ride…having dinner with my mom and Dad, talking and planning our next family vacation…having breakfast alone, my mom grief-stricken, my father dead…David's face as it pressed into mine during a kiss to mourn the loss of Jenna…David's face, lost and rejected as I yelled at him to leave me…Lance, handsome and glowing by the firelight, giving me moments of reprieve…friends incinerated…lives lost…the hope of sanctuary in a mountain out west…Claire staring at me with hatred…

Images of both suffering and reprieve haunted my sleep and kept me restless and unsteady. It was only Lance's voice that finally released me from their grip.

"Water," I heard him say.

I sat up with a start, shivering as my body was released from the warm covers. I looked around at the enormity of darkness surrounding us. I suddenly felt very small and insignificant.

"Water," he repeated, reminding me of our recent events and igniting my response.

Quickly I reached over to my left and found the candle and matches from the night before. I lit them so that I could see proof that my patient was still alive.

"Lance, you're okay?"

"Thirsty."

I felt his head with my ungloved hand. It was again burning hot with fever, yet his body was visibly shivering with chills. I gently lifted the bandages. Although his wound was no longer bleeding, it was incredibly swollen and looked red and hot. It was infected. His body was full of infection. He needed antibiotics. *What can I do now?* I wondered. I looked around at the emptiness of our surroundings. I didn't want to be left alone. I needed to take action. I needed to leave my cowardice in the past with everything else. I stood as I spoke.

"We don't have any water left, but I'll find you some. I just need a moment to figure out where." I picked up the maps that I had stolen from the cannibals' stand. Preparing to journey, I pressed the covers around Lance's body to try and keep him warm. Next I laid the road maps carefully along the flat ground. As I used my hands to smooth the paper, I noted the dried blood stains. I quickly dismissed their past, hardened in my call to the present. The maps were covered in hand-written notes and symbols. The words recorded names of towns and stores in the vicinity, with black X's marking certain areas. Using the maps and added annotations, I estimated that we were in a town named Valley Grove, West Virginia. If I could trust the killers' notes, we were in the thick of Castleman Run Wildlife Management Area. Using the scale, I estimated we were still fifteen miles or so from the next big city, Wheeling. That was too far. Lance wouldn't be able to make the journey. There had to be something closer. The nearest main artery was Castleman Road, Highway 53. We had to move. I had to get Lance help. Surely there would be a house or two somewhere around a main road. I noticed three black X's next to the highway. I guessed that the marks indicated that there was, or once was something there. It was time to find out. I folded up the maps and placed them into my left jacket pocket. Next, I walked off to ready myself for the journey. I relieved myself, adjusted my clothing, and then used the corner of my sweatshirt to rub the sleep from my eyes. I removed my hat and twisted the top of my long hair into a big knot, stuffing it inside of the hat. I hid my sin-stained hands inside of my black gloves and then wrapped my scarf tightly around my neck. Ready to make the move, I leaned down to gently speak to an ailing Lance.

"Lance, we have to go. We need to get you help."

"I can't," he weakly replied. "I can't make it."

"Yes you can," I insisted. "I found a location. It is only a mile away. You can do this. I will help you."

He shook his head no. He was not able, but I was. I had to get him to move. If I left him here, he would die.

"I can't leave you," I said.

The corners of his mouth curled into a small smile. "Does that mean you still care?" For an instant his face regained the handsome features that had first attracted me: the flirty smile, the chiseled cheekbones, the sparkling blue eyes.

I wasn't sure if I still cared or not, but I needed to encourage him in order to save him. "Yeah, I still care. Now come on. I'll help you. Once we get there we can get you some water and medicine." I removed his blankets and helped him to sit up. He was shivering with fever; we had to move fast. I rolled up my sleeping bag and attached it to my pack. I left his on the ground, as I could only carry one while I helped him walk. We would have to leave his behind. I placed our backpacks, one empty and one filled with only a rifle and our meager food supply, onto my back and then leaned down to help him rise. He winced at my touch and groaned in agony with his effort to stand. I allowed him to wrap his unharmed right shoulder around mine, and lean his body weight onto me. Together we set off to a main road and risked encountering some type of civilization, past or present.

We moved slowly through the woods. I kept my candle lit, its flame flickering with our slow pace. Even though the map claimed that Castleman Road was only a mile away, I feared the journey would take us an hour. *Maybe I should have left him behind. Maybe I could have made it safely to the house and back again in time.* But this was no time for regrets; we were on with our flight. I knew that Lance was in extreme pain, yet he was stoic, doing his best to silence his suffering. His weight upon me was burdensome; I could feel the responsibility for his life within my very marrow. I was sweating even in the post-apocalyptic winter. As I glanced around in the dim light of my candle, I saw no signs of civilization. The trees were mostly empty of leaves; the ground littered with detritus: dark, rotting, and void of life. There were no animals, no people. I wondered, *How many of us survived the explosion? How many made it through the weeks and months after?* Right now, it seemed like only Lance and I were left. I thought about David. *Was he still alive?* I tried to remember his face, but it kept fading from my memories: his long, dark hair; tall, lean frame; dark brown, melancholy eyes. I tried to picture the last time I saw him. It was the morning I left with Lance. He was sleeping by the dying embers of the fire, lying between Jared and Jack. He looked so peaceful as his eyes moved under their lids, probably full of his private dreams. How I longed to know their secrets. How I ached for his touch.

"Sarah," Lance winced. "I need to stop. I need water."

"I know Lance," I replied. "We're going to get you water, medicine, and rest. We have to be almost there. Lean all of your weight on me. I'll help you." But instead of leaning on me, he collapsed and fell to the ground.

"Lance!" I cried out to him. But there was no response. I knelt down beside his body and felt for his pulse. It was weak, but it was there. We still had probably a quarter mile to go. I took off my sleeping bag and laid it on top of him. Even though he was passed out, I placed the hunting rifle under his right arm. And then I snuffed out the candle and took off solo, heading east toward Castleman Road.

As I ran, the land became somewhat flatter. I stopped and ignited my lighter. There were few trees, and in the distance I could make out what appeared to be a clearing. I took off at a sprint; I had to be almost there. My feet began to beat hard on the ground and I could hear water underneath. I slowed down and flicked my light back on. I was crossing over a cement bridge. Ahead I could see the shadow of a building. Upon closer inspection I could see that it was a house. I was no longer on a bridge; I was on someone's driveway. Aware of the possible danger, I extinguished my light and walked slowly and silently. I took the small revolver from my coat pocket and held it in my right hand. I would no longer allow myself to be a victim.

As I approached the structure, I stopped to listen. I could hear no signs of life. I crept up next to the shadow of the house and approached the front door. It was big and dark, seemingly untouched and devoid of welcome. Maybe this house was one left untouched. After all, it was in the middle of nowhere. Maybe I had found the Grail of food and medicine. Maybe I could save us both. I readied the revolver in my right hand, while I slowly touched the doorknob with my left. It was then that I heard a clicking sound and felt something hard and cold pressed against my temple. It was the barrel of a gun.

7

Others

"Don't move or you're dead," the female voice said.

"She's got a weapon," a male added from behind. I felt someone grab my pistol and then rough and insensitive hands groping all parts of my body, searching for more weapons. They paused momentarily as they met with my swollen abdomen, and then abruptly carried on with the search. I immediately felt stripped of the little bit of humility I had left as I felt those hands remove everything from my person: the second revolver, the two maps, Rick's butcher knife, and my lighter.

"That's it, she's clean," said the male voice.

"You better be sure," said the female.

"Let's go," he replied angrily.

I felt rough fabric scratch my cheeks as a hood was forced over my head. My arms were jerked backwards

before one of my captors tied my hands with rope. I was
their prisoner. How would I be used this time? *Someone,
save me!* I thought. But I knew that I had no one to help me.
Strangely, I was not terrified; I was not even afraid. I was
just ready to calmly accept my fate, whatever it was to be.
Hands pushed me from behind.

"Walk," the male said. He kept one of his hands on
my right shoulder to guide me. With the existing darkness
and the added cover of the hood, I felt like I was being
readied to walk off of a cliff. Finally, we stopped. I heard a
creaking noise as the stranger's hand pushed down on my
head, forcing me to lean down into a crouch. He gave me a
shove and I crawled through what must have been a trap
door or secret entry of some type. Once inside, he used his
arms to return me to a standing position. I could see light
emanating through my mask, but still I did not panic. I did
not feel alone. I felt a presence within me. Someone took
off my hood. My eyes struggled to adjust to the space
illuminated by a small gas lantern. Slowly, as my vision
returned, I saw that I was in a large room with a small group
of people. There were five, three male and two female.

"Found her at the front door," the female from my
initial capture said. In the light I could see that she was
much smaller than her voice. She was of Asian descent, and
although young, probably not much older than I was, she
looked hardened by post-apocalyptic life. She took off her
hat to reveal short and spikey bleached-white hair poisoned
with the dark roots of neglect. To her left stood the male
who had searched me. He was tall and pale. Reddish-brown
curls peeked out from under his black woolen hat, and while
he was probably not any older than the girl, an established
beard made him look more authoritative. His eyes were on
mine, inquisitive in their search of my secrets. I met his

gaze with a blank stare that I was determined would give nothing away.

"Any weapons?" a deep voice asked from the back of the room.

"Yeah," the bearded male said while turning away from me and walking toward the back of the room. He placed my two small guns, knife, maps, and other meager possessions on top of a round table.

"You and Eva better get back to your post," the deep voice said. "We'll take it from here."

"Come on Marcus," I heard the Asian girl say, and then I watched as she and the bearded male, Marcus, left from my view. I turned toward the others while assessing my prison.

It was a large area, probably once a family room in a spacious home. The walls were a pale yellow and the floors a dark wood. It smelled stale and void of vigor. Looking downward, I saw pieces of abandoned existence here and there: empty food cans, empty wrappers, empty water bottles. Raising my eyes, I saw that the windows were covered and nailed shut with what looked like thick pieces of wood or old paneling. There was a huge stone fireplace in the middle of the back wall, yet no fire burned. In the back of the room, on the left, was the large round table that held my possessions. Suddenly standing next to me was the young male with the deep voice, handsome and dark-skinned, not much older than I; and in the center of the room next to two large brown sofas, stood my two other captors, a male and a female probably in their early twenties. They looked like they could have been college students or young professionals before all of this mess. I fixed my gaze upon them.

"Who are you?" the dark-skinned male standing next to me said. I turned and looked at him. He was so close that it startled me; I could see right into his eyes. They were filled with an air of strength and confidence, yet I sensed a softness that was lacking in my first two captors. I swallowed hard before I spoke.

"Sarah." My voice came out surprisingly strong and clear. Its music empowered me.

"Why are you here?" he asked.

I suddenly remembered my urgency. "My friend, he's hurt. He's been shot. He needs food, water, medicine."

"Where is he?" asked a tall female approaching me as she spoke.

"About a quarter of a mile west of here. He was too weak to travel."

"How did you know we were here?" asked the male leader by my side. I noticed that the second male, pale, tall and muscular, remained somewhat timid as he stood by the sofa remaining silent. Although he looked physically strong, his internal presence was weak. I looked away from him and answered the more confident male who was still standing next to me.

"I found some maps and noted the marks. They're over on the table." I pointed to the round table at the back of the room. "I assumed the markings indicated that there was something to find here."

" Look," I began to explain in a mixture of exhaustion and frustration, "I am of no danger to you. I just need to get help for my friend. He lost a lot of blood, and his wound is infected. If I don't get him some water and some antibiotics, he's going to die. Can you help me or not?" I couldn't believe my boldness.

After a moment or two of silence, someone spoke. It was the tall, young woman.

"Yes, we can help you," she said. The two others looked at her like they were surprised by her offer.

"Hadassah," the one next to me said.

"It's okay," Hadassah replied. "She's telling the truth." The others seemed to trust her judgment. She walked behind me and untied my arms. It was only after their release that I could feel the pain from their capture. She touched me gently on the left arm as she guided me over to one of the sofas.

"Sit." I sat down on the firm cushion while Hadassah remained standing. She was tall and thin with long black hair and large green eyes. Her young face had something unique about it; I guess if discernment were a physical characteristic, then that is what her face beheld. She looked like she never panicked, like she always knew what action to take.

"Paul," she said to the deep-voiced male who had first spoken to me. Get Sarah something to eat and drink. I'll get some meds."

Paul walked toward the fireplace. He was dark-skinned and lean, with cropped hair held firmly in tight curls. He reached inside and pulled out a large box. He opened it and gathered some of its contents. Next he walked over and handed me a bottle of water and a can of food. I looked at the label; it was wet cat food. At first I hesitated, but then I reluctantly opened the can. It looked and smelled like tuna and I hadn't eaten in days. Before I could reconsider, I devoured it, and God was it good. Our pets didn't know how good they had it, and the reality is that neither did we. It was only as I tipped the water bottle to my mouth and felt its streams spilling along my cheeks, that I took hold of my appearance. I must have resembled an animal to them.

"Sorry," I said. "It's been a long time since…" Hadassah walked back into the room. She placed a small pill bottle in my hands. It looked so normal, a relic of our old lives. I read the label: Samuel Maddox, 1000 Garrison Run Road, Valley Grove, West Virginia. I wondered where Samuel Maddox was now. Was he alive or dead? I again looked at the bottle and read the instructions; Amoxicillin, take one tablet two times per day.

This is it, I thought. *This could save him.*

"Thank you," I whispered. "I've got to get this to him right away. I stuffed the pills into my pocket along with my half-full bottle of water. "I've got to go."

"Wait," said Paul. "Hadassah," he continued as he looked directly at the young woman, "we need to talk." I watched as their eyes met. I could see that they had a connection, that they completely trusted one another. She and the timid male walked over to meet him. They tried to whisper, but I could hear their heated words.

"How do we know we can trust her? She could just be luring the others to us."

What others? I thought.

"No," Hadassah said.

"What makes you so sure?"

"I see it in her eyes," Hadassah said. "She is still human, not like the others. She is still one of us."

I watched as Paul sighed. "Mitch," he said. You stay here and finish your rest assignment. I'll go with Hadassah and make sure the situation is secure." Mitch nodded and headed back toward the sofa where I assume he had been sleeping before my arrival. I guess they took shifts, resting and guarding the house. But guarding it from what, exactly, I was not sure. I watched as Paul leaned over and gently kissed Hadassah's lips.

"You're going to be the death of me," I heard him tell her. Then they began piling on their coats, hats, and scarves as they readied to join me in my journey. As we set off in my hope to save Lance, I replayed Hadassah's troubling words in my thoughts: *She is still human, not like the others; she is still one of us.* Who were they afraid of? If these 'others' were not human, then what were they?

8

Judas

I knew I didn't have time to ponder a zombie apocalypse or any other type of fiction; I had to get back to reality, to Lance, and I had to do it fast. Paul looked at Hadassah and gave a nod. It was time to go.

"I'm sorry," he said, as he again placed the hood over my head. He led me toward the back of the house somewhere, but he was much gentler than my original captors had been.

"The front door is nailed shut. We keep our true entrance a secret," said Hadassah. "I'm sure you understand."

I didn't understand, of course, but didn't have time to think about it now.

"We're here," Paul said. "Lean down Sarah and then crawl forward." I did as he commanded, and quickly felt the cool air hit my body. One of them helped me to rise, and then walked me toward what I assumed was the front of the house. I heard rustling noises.

"One," Paul yelled, I assumed to alert Eva and Marcus who were standing outside on guard. "We're taking her back to find her friend." He took off my hood. I was standing where I had first met with their front line of defense, a gun pressed into the side of my head. I decided it was best to keep quiet and let Paul and Hadassah speak for me.

"You sure about this?" Marcus asked.

"No," Paul confessed, "but Hadassah is." I heard the other male let out a small laugh. Eva stared me down with distrust, like she was trying to find something in my outer appearance that would reveal an abnormal or dangerous inner character.

"It's okay," said Hadassah, meeting Eva's eyes. She then reached out and placed her hands on both of Eva's shoulders. "She's one of us. We're going with her, to find her companion. He's hurt. He needs our help." Eva gave a reluctant nod.

"Be safe," Marcus said.

As we hurried away from the entrance to their house, I tried to get my bearings. We needed to cross the cement driveway and then head straight west to the Castleman Run Wildlife Area. Lance was only about a quarter of a mile into the woodlands. I went to reach for my lighter and realized that it, along with all of my weapons-- my knife and my guns--was gone. Without them I felt vulnerable.

"Where to?" Paul asked.

Standing still, I closed my eyes and tried to sense my path. I lifted my arms away from the earth as I searched. And then, I felt it. The pull of purpose led me. I took off running away from my captors and toward my companion. I felt Paul and Hadassah's presence close behind me. I did not fear them. I did not fear stumbling and falling. I did not fear anything except Lance's death. I continued until I saw a large bundle on the ground. It was Lance. He had not moved. I hoped my greatest fear was not realized.

"Lance," I yelled frantically. "Lance." I gently shook him and tapped his face with my hands. Hadassah and Paul quickly knelt down beside me. There was no movement, no life. I picked up his right hand and felt for a pulse. It was there. I placed my cheek next to his mouth and although it was soft and shallow, breath was there. I looked up at Hadassah and Paul.

"He's alive," I said.

Hadassah leaned over and felt his head. "Where was he shot?"

I lowered the blanket and raised Lance's sweater above his left shoulder. The three of us stared at his very infected wound.

"We need to get medicine into him now," Hadassah said firmly.

She and Paul got behind Lance and lifted him up into a seated position. I grabbed the bottle of water and pills from my coat pocket. Using my hands, I forced Lance's mouth open. I placed my fingers into his mouth and opened the pathway to his throat. I strategically placed a pill down inside, as deeply as I could reach. Grabbing the half-filled water bottle I had carried from the house, I quickly unscrewed the cap and forced some water into Lance's mouth as Hadassah and Paul reclined his head to force the pill downward and into the depths of his throat. He began to choke. He coughed and gasped and it brought him back to us. It brought him back to me.

"Lance!" I shouted. "Lance!"

He looked at me with confused eyes. He didn't know who I was or where he was for that matter.

"Lance, it's me Sarah!"

Slowly, his gaze began to sharpen and come together on my face. His eyes appeared to melt as they met mine.

"Sarah," he said. "You came back."

"Of course I did," I said. Then he looked at me in such a way, that I knew that while he may have lied about many things, he did not lie about the fact that he loved me. It softened me.

"Yes, I'm back," I said. My words meant more than he could have realized.

He alerted to the two strangers who were with me. Recognizing that he was too weak to speak, Hadassah moved in front of him so that he could directly see her.

"Lance," she said, "My name is Hadassah. This is Paul. We are no danger to you or Sarah. We are here to help you."

Lance looked into my eyes for reassurance. I wasn't entirely sure if we were safe, but I gave him a nod that would let him rest in thinking so. He smiled softly as he fought to keep his eyes open. Hadassah looked at his feeble condition, and then at me. I must have looked like a wreck too, because I saw raw sympathy in her eyes. She sighed and then softly spoke.

"You can both come back to the safe house. You can stay with us."

"Hadassah," Paul said sharply.

"They need our help," she replied.

"We need to check with the others first," Paul said.

"Coming with us is his only chance. They can stay with us until he is well. We can at least offer that."

Hadassah was right. Lance and I didn't have a chance out here. We had no food, no water, no way to protect ourselves.

"We won't stay long," I said. "We have a destination. We're headed southeast."

Hadassah gave me a puzzled look.

"We still need to check with the others," Paul said.

Hadassah nodded. I gave Lance two more pills, which he quickly swallowed with the last of my water, knowing that their healing powers were his only path back toward life. After what seemed like a half hour or so, we helped Lance to stand. He kept one arm around me and one around Paul. As we headed off into the darkness and toward the safe house, Lance leaned heavily onto me. I struggled to continue, but pursued, because he was alive. After four months of seeing and experiencing unspeakable things, we were both still alive, and I found my burden lightened with hope. And then I smiled to myself, remembering that deep within I truly was filled with Hope. My own little Hope. With all of the distractions of surviving, I had forgotten to live. I focused intensely, and sure enough, although slight, I felt her. As she moved inside of me, I suddenly began to feel somewhat disoriented, yet at the same time focused with clarity, like I could see the bridge that separated the natural world from the supernatural. And then they came, just like they always did at these moments, strange words of guidance or warning: "Beware of your friends; do not trust your clan, for there is a deceiver." And then it was over. And as we neared the safe house, I wondered how safe we really were, and who was going to be the Judas this time.

9

Dreams

"One and two," Hadassah called out.

"Password?" a voice shouted.

"Colorado," she replied.

Colorado, I thought. But I didn't have time to ask. As we approached what I had learned was the "mock" front entrance to the safe house, I saw that Mitch had taken over guard duty from Eva and Marcus. He was standing on alert, waiting for us.

"Do we really need to do this?" asked Hadassah as Mitch handed her two old hoods with which to cover our heads.

"We don't know enough about them yet," answered Paul.

Hadassah nodded, relinquishing her concerns to the obvious trust she held in Paul. She looked apologetically into my eyes. "Sorry Sarah."

She handed me the hood while she took my place holding Lance's right side. I voluntarily placed it over my head and waited to be guided toward the secret entrance. I felt someone gently place their hand around my left arm and lead me down the now familiar path. I probably could have found the entrance without their lead. After a short while I heard Hadassah's voice, "Okay Sarah, lean down and crawl through." I obeyed, and in no time, smelled the stale and familiar air of the safe house. Realizing Hadassah had not even tied my arms, I removed my hood and found myself standing in the dark.

"Who's here?" I heard a male voice yell. Immediately the gas lantern flared and I saw Eva and Marcus standing by the sofa on the left side of the room, their guns pointed at my head.

"It's okay," Hadassah quickly yelled from the back of the house. "One and two returning with the victims."

It was not long before I saw Hadassah and Paul carrying Lance into the room, laying him on the sofa sitting across from the others. It looked like he had again fallen unconscious. I walked quickly to his side. He looked at me with half-opened eyes and smiled.

"Sarah," he whispered. He was weak, but he was awake.

"Where are you going to put them?" Marcus asked.

"They can stay in Kelly's room," I heard Hadassah say.

"What? Are you really ready to…"

"Marcus," Hadassah said. "She is gone."

"It just seems wrong," he answered.

"I know it's hard," Paul said while approaching them, "but we need to move on."

I watched Marcus angrily lower himself to the sofa. Eva sat down next to him and lifted his arm, placing it on her lap in an attempt to comfort him. It was obvious that this group had experienced loss, as had I.

"A little help?" Paul asked Marcus. Reluctantly, Marcus stood and helped Paul lift Lance off of the sofa. Hadassah, who had picked up the gas lantern, turned and nodded for me to follow. They led me through a vacant kitchen and into a hallway with four doors, two on each side. We entered through the second door on the right. It was a small room; we could barely fit inside. Hadassah placed the lamp on the small nightstand next to a double bed, pushed up against a darkly paneled wall. Paul and Marcus carefully lay Lance on the far side of the bed. Lance made some light moaning noises, but otherwise remained pretty incoherent. Marcus gave me a quick and expressionless glance, and then he and Paul abruptly left the room.

"You must be exhausted," Hadassah said. She lifted the lantern, and replaced it with a small candle. Next she placed a jar half-full of nuts or seeds of some kind and two full water bottles on the nightstand.

"There is running water in the bathroom just outside of your door to the right. Please don't leave your room except to use it. The others may take you for an intruder and shoot you. I will come and check on you later. In the meantime, if you need anything, just knock hard on this wall (she pointed to the one behind the bed). You would be surprised how the noise travels in this house. And Sarah," she added with a concerned look, "know that you two can stay as long as he needs."

"Thank you," I said. I had many questions that I wanted to ask her, but for now I was way too tired, and I was sitting on a real bed. All I needed was sleep, a good and long sleep. I watched as she slowly walked out of the room, closing the door behind her. Alone in the space, I better surveyed our surroundings. Other than the bed and the nightstand, the room was empty. The one small window to my left was nailed shut with wood paneling, and the bed lacked any sheets or blankets. I got up and slowly detached my sleeping bag from my pack. Unfolding it, I shook off the leaves and twigs from my outdoor living experience, then climbed onto the bed and lay the now more civilized cover on top of Lance and me. I touched him on the forehead. He was warm, but breathing steadily in his sleep. He was all that I knew now, all that was familiar and secure, and he did love me. I lifted his uninjured right arm and pressed my body under it and against his side. I placed my hands on top of Hope, thinking that the gesture of warmth would help her, too, to feel secure. And then, in exhaustion, I fell into a deep sleep, one only interrupted, hours later, by a single, vivid, and terrifying dream.

In the dream I was being chased, running and running with all of my strength. I knew that I was in grave danger, but I didn't know who or what was behind me. It was them. I couldn't see anything, but the presence was definitely a "them," and they were coming for me. I could feel their danger closing in. I looked up in desperation and I saw a light. It was Hadassah. She was holding the gas lantern. "Run!" she screamed. "Over here! Run, Sarah!" I felt her energy fill me as I ran toward her. The light grew brighter and brighter as I neared her secure presence.

"You did it Sarah," she said as I fell safely at her feet. "I knew you could do it. Colorado is not so far." I looked up at her, trying to catch my breath. I knew that she had saved me, but I didn't know how. As I looked up to thank her, I saw her upper body jar with movement. The lantern crashed to the ground and the light it gave was gone. And then Hadassah fell down on the ground next to me. And she was dead.

10

Reflections

I awoke with a gasp and abruptly sat up in bed. Where was I? I looked around. The candle next to my side was still lightly flickering. I took a deep breath. The nightstand, the boarded up window, the double bed, Lance. I was in the safe house. I was safe, if only for now. My heart was racing and I was covered in a thin layer of sweat.

"Sarah." It was Lance. "Where are we?"

I tried to gain control of my emotions as I turned toward him. I didn't want to frighten him.

"It's okay Lance, we're safe," I said in an attempt to both calm myself and assure him of his security. I gently placed my hand on his forehead. It was again hot.

"What happened?" he asked.

"You were shot. Do you remember?"

I watched as he tried to process all that had happened in the past days, or was it weeks? Time was losing its meaning as I was losing my control of its passing.

"Yeah, I remember," he said. "You took the bullet out. I definitely remember that." He smiled as he turned to look at me. For a brief moment, his face looked young, innocent, and free of the mess we were in.

"Yes, I did," I said smiling back. "Do you remember anything else?"

"No."

"Your wound got infected. I had to get help. I found other people. Good people. We are with them now. We are staying in their safe house."

"Safe house?" he asked.

"They take turns guarding it against others." I went on to explain some of the things I had observed, but soon realized that Lance had fallen back to sleep.

There was a light knock at the door.

"Sarah?"

"Come in."

Hadassah gently opened the door and walked into the room.

"Just came in to check on you. Everything okay?"

"Yeah, thanks," I said.

"How's he doing?" she asked.

"About the same," I admitted.

Hadassah breathed deeply. "Why don't you go out and spend some time with the others. I can sit with him for a while." Glad to leave the tiny room, I agreed.

"Thanks," I said as I turned to go.

"Sarah, wait. When you enter the main room, announce yourself. Say 'Four.'"

I thought about the person who used to occupy this room. "Was four *her* number?"

J.E.Byrne

"Yes," she said. "Her name was Kelly." Hadassah handed me a candle for light. I looked up at her, and then slowly walked out of the room and closed the door.

I decided to make an attempt with the others; perhaps they could provide a distraction. Besides, I had questions for them, and I'm sure they had some for me.

"Four," I yelled as I approached the main room. The lantern was still burning, throwing off jittery shadows throughout the room. Eva and Marcus were sitting on one of the large sofas and looked up at me, seemingly shocked that I could be so bold as to take on Kelly's number.

"How dare you," bit Eva. I watched as Marcus used his arm to hold her down on the sofa. I think she was about to leap up and punch me.

"Sorry," I said. "Hadassah told me to say four so that you would know I wasn't an intruder."

"She shouldn't have done that," Eva said under her breath.

"Is it okay if I sit?" I asked. My heart was trembling underneath of my sweatshirt. Here I was in a post-apocalyptic world with other survivors, and yet I felt just as insecure and ridiculous as if I were back in a crowded high school cafeteria asking if I could sit at the table with the cool kids.

"Of course," said Marcus. "Sarah, right?" he asked, trying to break the tension.

"Yeah."

"What do you want?" asked Eva.

"I don't want anything," I replied. "I just came out to, ya know, thank you for letting Lance and me stay here for a while, until we are able to travel again."

"Where were you going?" asked Marcus.

I looked up at him as I began to answer. With his hat off he looked more fragile than I had first noticed. His auburn

66

hair was long and all pushed back from his high forehead. His eyes, green or blue, looked lost and troubled. Beneath his coarse beard was just a young man who was scared and trying to hold it all together, just like I was; just like we all were I guessed.

"Lance and I were headed south. We wanted to make it to the coast, maybe the Carolinas or Georgia, before winter. We're hoping it'll be warmer there – that the ocean will still hold some living food."

"That's where we're headed too," Marcus said. "We're actually hoping to make it to Florida."

"Then why are you staying here?" I asked. Eva looked up. Unlike Marcus, her eyes were flat and cold.

"Why are *you* here?" she asked.

"Lance was shot," I answered. "I came for help."

"Who shot him?" she asked.

"A man and a woman from the woods. I think they were living there. I found what I believe was their shelter."

"Why'd they shoot him?'

"They wanted to kill us both." I swallowed. "They wanted to *eat* us both."

"Oh God," she murmured. "Corpses."

"What do you mean *corpses*?" I asked.

"That's what we call the losers who've chosen survival over humanity," she said.

"And you haven't?" I asked somewhat relieved.

"Of course not!" Eva added. "What happened to them – the man and woman?"

"We killed them," I said. "But don't worry," I added, "we didn't eat them."

With my comment, the ice melted, and Eva burst out laughing. I smiled, but at the same time thought about the man and woman – how their eyes looked soulless; they were like the walking dead. I suddenly understood why some people adhered to all of the zombie stories. It really wasn't all that far from the realm of possibility.

"How'd you kill them?" Eva asked.

"Lance shot the man," I said. "I shot the woman."

"Good," Eva nodded as she looked directly at me. It appeared as though I had earned her respect as she was able to see me as a fellow survivor and not a agitating splinter – a blight in their finely tuned group.

"We're here because of them." she said. "The corpses. Marcus and I were travelling through Wheeling when we were ambushed by a group of them. We fought as best as we could, but there were too many of them. That's when we met Hadassah, Paul, and Mitch. They were hiding in the woods. They came to our aid and together, the five of us killed them. We killed them all and left them for other corpses to munch away on. Karma, I say. This was their house. We found Kelly in here, tied up and held prisoner in the back room – your room. As you can imagine, she was in pretty bad shape." Eva looked down at the floor. I guess she wasn't as tough as she put on.

"We tried to save her," Marcus said, picking up where Eva left off. "She seemed like she was recovering. We thought she'd be okay. Mitch, he stayed with her, wouldn't leave her side. One night, she picked up his pistol; he had left it on the table next to the bed. We all heard the shot."

"You mean she killed herself?" I asked.

"Yeah," Marcus answered. "Mitch hasn't spoken much since."

"I'm sorry," I said. I could see that sharing this story with me was their way of accepting me. It mattered to both of them. And I felt a tugging. Even though I didn't know Kelly, it also mattered to me.

"We decided to stay here for a week or so to replenish supplies and get some rest before making our journey south," Marcus added.

"You and Lance can come with us," Eva said as she looked up at me, her dark eyes peering from beneath her spiked bangs. I saw Marcus's face soften as she clasped his hand. The two of them held a bond – were a part of the other.

"Thanks," I said. "I'd like that."

"One," Paul announced as he entered the room from somewhere in the back. We all jumped up.

"You're all dead," he added.

"Sorry Paul," Marcus said. "We were talking with Sarah. Won't happen again."

"Better not," said Paul. "No more losses – isn't that our creed?"

"Yeah," said Eva as she smiled at me. "No more losses. Sarah's coming with us Paul."

"Really," Paul said as he looked at me. "Where's Hadassah?"

"She's with Lance," I said. "I'll head back and get her. I stood and began to make my way to our room, the one where someone named Kelly had been both rescued and lost.

After making it through the kitchen, I stopped in the small bathroom outside of the room. I figured it could be hours before I again left the tiny bedroom. I placed the candle on the left side of the sink and peered into the mirror. I was careful to observe that my eyes still reflected my humanity. I would end my own life before I'd allow myself to lose all hope and turn into a corpse. I wondered if that's what happened to Kelly. If she worried that she would turn into a reflection of one of them. I studied the worn, thin woman staring back. She had dark circles and sunken cheeks. She could really use some Botox. I smiled to myself for the first time in, well, several weeks. I found a small piece of soap on the sink. I turned on the faucet to allow some cold water to flow. I lathered up the tiny piece of soap and smothered my face with its bubbles. I even ran the bubbles over my teeth and the inside of my mouth. I scrubbed and scrubbed as if it could take this whole nightmare away, but of course it didn't. I rinsed my mouth and face, allowing the black water to run down the drain until it eventually cleared. I looked around and saw a small tan towel on a rack to the right side of the sink. It had small white daisies with yellow centers embroidered along its border. How insignificant, and yet so lovely, such details now seemed. I lifted the towel and patted my face dry, on the part above the flowers. I didn't want to spoil their beauty. I wondered how the others saw me now. Did Hadassah see me as one to be pitied? Did Eva and Marcus view me as a heartless killer? I looked back at my reflection and tried to remember how I looked before.

I thought back to the night of Derek's party, the night of my fiery baptism. I closed my eyes, trying to recall the normalcy of everything before. I remembered getting out of the shower that night, in my own bathroom at home. I remembered staring at my reflection then too, also wondering how others saw me. I wondered if Derek would think I was pretty enough. I wondered if Chelsea and Alex would think I looked cool enough. I wondered if my mom would think I looked good enough, and yet others, brave or strong enough. I never really looked at myself and just saw who I honestly was. Maybe that was because I didn't know who I was.

I rinsed my face and my teeth and looked one last time at my reflection. And who was I now? The strange words came again: "You are my workmanship." This time the words did not confuse me. Being someone's work in progress felt right. I smiled at my reflection. My outer beauty was fading, but inwardly I was growing stronger each day. I lifted my layers of clothing and looked down. My swollen belly reminded me of my determination to survive. The bathroom mirror was too small for me to see my reflection below my chest, so I opened the door and walked into the hall. Again I lifted my heavy clothes and stood on my toes so that I could see the proof of Hope. Sure enough, my reflection mirrored her presence. Suddenly the small door to the bedroom flew open and Hadassah ran out and almost into me. Left completely vulnerable, Hadassah froze as she took in my obvious pregnant state. I quickly covered myself, embarrassed to have my secret exposed, but she didn't seem to focus on it. There was something even more pressing.

"Sarah," she said, "you need to get in here right away." And then she led me into the bedroom and over to where Lance was thrashing about and moaning strange and barely conceivable words:

I didn't mean it. It wasn't supposed to happen. I shouldn't have taken you Sarah. I know. It's wrong. I know. I'm sorry. So sorry. Leah! It wasn't supposed to happen. No! Stop it! No one was supposed to get hurt! Stop, no! I shouldn't have taken you Sarah. No one was supposed to get hurt! I know it's wrong! I know. I know. I know. She's dead. She's dead. Leah's dead. I'm so sorry. So sorry. so sorry. Sarah, I'm so sorry...

And then he fell back asleep.

"What's he saying?" Hadassah asked as she noticed the tears running down my face.

"Confirmation of things I already knew but didn't want to face," I said.

She nodded. "You're pregnant."

"Yes," I said as I wiped my tears.

"My God," she said.

"Yes, my God," I replied. And then I realized how my reflection must have looked to Hadassah…pretty hopeless.

11

Truth

"Do you want to talk about it?" Hadassah asked.

"I'm not sure," I confessed. I had held in my thoughts and feelings for so long, my whole life really, that I wasn't sure if I could share them with her. I was afraid to be exposed. I had only ever opened up to two others, Jenna, who left me in her death, and David, who left me in both his decision to stay with Claire, and in my insistence that he leave me. I had been such a fool in telling him that I loved him. It felt like my skin had been ripped off, exposing me for the fragile girl that I truly was. I didn't like being vulnerable; as far as I could tell, it only led to excruciating pain.

"No, I'm okay," I lied. But Hadassah was different. She was discerning.

"No you're not," she said.

I hardened my face in an attempt to look stoic, but the action did not fool her.

"How about I reveal something to you about myself first?" she asked.

I nodded. I was curious to learn something about this perceptive young woman who lived in this stifling safe house. Why was she here? What was her plan for the future? Did she even have one, or was she just following the others, planning to head south in hopes of warmth, hoping to not be overtaken by some supposedly non-human others? And then there was her strange password...Colorado. What did she know about Colorado?

"Paul found me," she began. "After, when I had given up all hope and was eagerly awaiting my death, he found me. He brought me back. He helped me to see that I was not left alive due to luck, but for a purpose. He more than rescued me; he saved me."

"Where did he find you?" I asked.

"Curled up in a fetal position and dying as a coward in a small and dirty corner of a hospital waiting room."

"Were you inside of the hospital when it happened?"

"No," she replied. "It happened just as I stepped outside to grab some fresh air and a quick work break. I mean imagine such a ridiculous thing, saved by some random decision," she said as she stared off into space seemingly searching for its significance.

"Are you a doctor?" I asked. Maybe this was why she had antibiotics and seemed to know how to care for Lance and me.

"I was an ER nurse," she continued. "The great irony," she said as she looked down into her hands that were folded in her lap, "was that I was trained to handle crisis situations. And yet, in the real crisis of finding everyone inside incinerated, I failed."

Hadassah raised her eyes from her hands and looked at me. Her honest words laid herself out, bare and open. She suddenly seemed quite vulnerable, like a young deer when it first senses your presence.

"Sarah," she said slowly and softly, "I grabbed a vial of narcotics. I opened the lid, and without more than a cowardly wish to forget all that I saw, I swallowed them. I swallowed them all. And then I curled up in a corner of the emergency room waiting area, and I waited to die."

"But you didn't," I whispered. "You didn't die."

"No, I didn't."

"What happened?" I asked, completely engaged in her story.

"Paul happened," she said.

"What did he do?" I asked.

"Paul and Mitch were EMT's. They, too, were outside on hospital grounds during the explosion. Like me, upon regaining consciousness, they entered the hospital trying to find out what happened. Like me, they were met with utter death and destruction; but unlike me, they did not surrender. Instead, they searched each section of the hospital, including one corner with a human still intact, still barely alive. By the time they found me, I had already drifted off into what I had hoped would be my eternal slumber. They saw the empty vial. They got to work and forced me awake, forced me to vomit my poison, forced me to live. Although I didn't personally know them, I recognized their faces. Barely scraping myself off of the floor, I ashamedly looked up at them both, vomit dribbling along my chin. I was mortified. I cursed them both; I mean, why would they bring me to such a pathetic state? Why would I even want to live when everyone else was dead?

I could see tears forming in the corners of Hadassah's eyes. She paused as they pooled and eventually trickled down her cheeks.

"I demanded that they leave. I assured them that I would just swallow more pills. But then Paul spoke and his words changed my heart. They changed it forever."

"What did he say?" I asked, slightly embarrassed to be privy to such raw and personal information.

"He told me that he loved me."

My heart sank. I knew those words. I had heard them from both David and from Lance, and they hurt as much as they healed. But Hadassah's story was different; she was still with the man she loved.

Hadassah continued, "I looked at Paul like he was irrational, because I didn't even know his name. I screamed at him, telling him that he was crazy and to just go away and leave me alone. But he didn't. Instead he picked me up off of the floor and stared right into my eyes. He told me how he had watched me in the ER, how he admired my strength and the way that I treated the patients and cared for them. He told me that it was not yet time for me to die, and so he would not allow it. He told me that it was not just a random coincidence that we had both survived, but that maybe we were spared now, so that later we could be used to save others."

"That's a tall order," I said.

Hadassah continued, "Yes. But saving others...wasn't that what I did for a living? Wasn't that my calling? I surrendered. I gave Paul my outstretched arm. He gently accepted it and then the three of us quietly walked out of the hospital and into whatever our remainder of life called us to do. And I think one of them was to find you."

I took a deep breath. Hadassah had bravely bared her soul in confessing her lowest moment, the one in which she tried and failed to take her own life. Her authenticity softened me.

"Hadassah," I confessed. "I've made a terrible mess out of everything. I don't know even which way to turn." With my confession, I broke down into tears. She reached over and placed her arms around me. I allowed myself to break under her embrace.

"It's okay," she said. "Everything will be okay."

"How can it be okay?" I sobbed. "The way I see it nothing will ever be okay again." I was losing my cool. I could feel my sense of control melting in waves around me. Hadassah distracted me with more questions.

"Why don't you start with telling me what happened," she said. "How did you end up here with Lance? Who shot him? And holy shit, Sarah, how far along are you?" she asked as she stared at my abdomen, now securely concealed under my clothing. "Paul, Mitch and I, we're a medical team. We can help you." She looked at Lance. "All *three* of you."

"It happened the day after the explosion," I began.

"What happened?" she asked.

"I was raped."

Hadassah gasped as she glared at Lance.

"No, it wasn't him." She looked away from him and back toward me. "I didn't know them," I added.

"Them?" she asked.

"Yes, them," I said in a soft voice.

"Sarah," Hadassah whispered, "I'm so sorry that happened to you."

I closed my eyes and continued out loud with my thoughts. "I'm guessing that it's late August or early September," I said, "so I must be somewhere between four and five months pregnant." I cringed when I heard myself say the word, even though nestled within it was reason for me to keep living.

"Have you been okay? Have you experienced any complications?" she asked.

"No. I mean, I was incredibly sick for a long time, but I guess that's somewhat normal." *Normal* I thought. *What even is normal anymore?* Shaking my head out of its distracting thoughts I continued, "Before I knew that I was pregnant, I thought I had some type of cancer. I'm still not always certain if my symptoms are from being pregnant, or if they're from just living in this dying world."

"Have you felt any movement?"

"Yes." I paused a moment before baring myself further. "If you want to, you can touch her. I mean, you can put your hands on me and feel her."

"You know she is a *her*?" Hadassah asked through a smile.

"Yes," I replied. "Her name is Hope." With this revelation, I lifted my ragged clothing and fully disclosed my secret to Hadassah. She placed her hands on me and waited for movement. It wasn't long before life kicked into Hadassah's hands. I watched as her face lit up with Hope's promise.

"So what should I do now?" I asked.

"You should stay with us. We can take care of you until your time comes. We can deliver her with you and be sure that you will both be safe."

"You and Paul are heading south with the others?" I asked.

"Mitch, Marcus, and Eva want to make it to Florida in search of warmer weather."

"But you're not so sure," I asked, hoping to question her 'Colorado' password.

"I feel this strange pull to head west," she said. "The others tease me. They nicknamed me 'Colorado.' Paul," she said with a slight smile, "he said he'll go wherever I choose."

"I was once headed west," I said. She looked up at me with interest.

"Why did you change your mind?" she asked.

"I think I lost my way," I replied.

"I think I did too," she said.

We both sat quietly for a few minutes, each contemplating our paths. I suddenly felt the need to correct mine. While a part of me wanted to stay with them, to be protected during Hope's birth, I knew that I couldn't. There was more to my story. There were matters involving a mountain, a boy named Jack, a love named David, a liar named Lance, and a murderer of Leah, and I inherently knew that Earth's clock was ticking, and the time for resolution was at hand.

'I can't stay," I said.

"Why not?" she asked.

"There's so much more to my story."

"I've got time."

I shifted uncomfortably on the corner of the bed where I was sitting. I wasn't sure how much more I wanted to reveal. I glanced over at Lance. In the dim light, he appeared to be sleeping soundly. The slight sounds of his breath were soft and his eyes were sealed tightly under the tufts of his blonde hair. Next I looked at Hadassah. Up close, she looked a little older than I had first thought. She had a few small lines in the middle of her forehead and the very beginnings of markings along the outer corners of her green eyes. "How old are you?" I asked her.

"Twenty-six," she replied. "How old are you?"

"Eighteen," I said. "But I feel like I'm eighty." I forced a small laugh before once again becoming serious. I took comfort in knowing that she was a bit older than I. Maybe with a few more years, she had a few more life experiences. And just maybe they could allow her to better understand the long life of poor choices and failed experiences I had quickly accumulated in these past months. I decided to risk the truth.

"We were travelling with others," I began. "Eleven others when I left."

"Are they...?" she hesitated.

"No," I quickly replied. "Well, one is."

"I betrayed them," I said.

"How?" She asked. She looked concerned with what I might reveal.

I continued, "They were counting on me. I know this is going to sound ridiculous, but we were headed to a mountain in Colorado." Hadassah gave me a strange look.

"Colorado?" she asked.

I decided to backtrack and explain. "After it all happened, the explosion and my assault, I was found by two other survivors, Rick and his son Jack. After Rick became sick and died, Jack and I stayed together. One night, we both shared a dream of a place we felt we were being led to. It was a mountain, huge and rocky; we assumed it was in Colorado. Later, while on the way, we met up with others: David, Claire, Jenna, Ruth, Britney, Katie, and Jared. They were headed to the same place; some had shared the same dream." Hadassah looked like she wanted to say something, but I was on a cathartic role and decided to keep going.

"We struggled. We lost Katie first, then Jenna, but eventually gained Ruth." I spoke to Hadassah as if she already knew them. "They became my family. David and I, we...I..." My face grew hot, my cheeks flushed. I looked away. It was too painful; I couldn't continue.

"You loved him." Hadassah said.

"Yes."

"Did he love you?"

"Yes."

"Why did you leave him?"

"There was another, Claire. He was with her when I met him. He had always been with her, before I mean. I forced him to choose, or thinking back, maybe I forced him to leave. I'm not sure anymore." I found myself drifting away for a moment, back to the time when David stayed with me for weeks, back to the time when he nursed me back to life. I told him I loved him. He told me that he loved me. *What happened? How did it all go wrong?*

"So what happened?" Hadassah brought my thoughts back to the present, to this room with a tiny candlelit night table, a badly wounded Lance, and a feeling of regret and loss.

"Soon after," I continued, "our group met up with Lance and his sister Leah. They were looking for help; Leah was sick. They joined our group. It was after I had told David to leave me and go back to Claire. David didn't fight for me then, and so I gave up on him; I gave up on us. I felt rejected, so hurt and all alone. Suddenly there was a new distraction. Lance was handsome and funny. He flirted with me. He treated me like I was the only one who mattered. It felt good; being with him lessened the hurt."

"Do you love him?" Hadassah asked. I looked over at Lance, ashamed to admit the truth.

"No," I said.

"Then why did you leave with him?"

"You shared your lowest point with me, right?" I said meeting Hadassah's eyes.

J.E.Byrne

"Yes," she replied.

"Well," I admitted, "mine was in leaving with Lance. It was after David heard me say that I was pregnant. He looked so confused, so shocked; he saw my half undressed, swollen, and ugly body about to have sex with Lance. In my need for love and acceptance, in all of my insecurities, I made a mess of everything. I figured that I had lost him forever. After, I was so ashamed. I couldn't face him or any of the others either. How would they understand? How could they?

"Didn't you tell David the truth? Sarah it wasn't your fault."

"It doesn't matter," I said.

"Of course it matters!" Hadassah raised her voice. "Being raped was not your fault. Being pregnant now is nothing to be ashamed of. You were a victim. Do you get that? You did nothing wrong! And if you love this man, and if he truly loves you, then you owe each other the truth."

I thought back to the moments before I left. I remembered how he spent the night relentlessly searching for me. Even after he saw my pregnant body, even after he saw me with Lance, he pursued; he would not give up. But I told him to leave me. I ordered him to go. I hid from him in my shame. Before I snuck away later that night, I saw him sleeping by the fire. He was next to Jack and Jared. Claire was not there. *Wait, Claire was not there!* I wondered what he wanted so desperately to tell me, what I wouldn't let him say. Hadassah was right. We owed *each other* the truth. My silence had hurt him as badly, perhaps even worse than he had hurt me. I realized that I loved him enough to risk everything. And at that moment I believed that he loved me enough to risk everything. I had to find him. I had to leave.

"Sarah," Hadassah again interrupted my thoughts. "I'm confused about what Lance was saying in his sleep.

82

You make it sound like you left with him voluntarily, yet he kept saying he was sorry that he took you away. That no one was supposed to get hurt, that no one was supposed to die."

Her questions helped me to connect once disjointed pieces. I again thought back to that last night. Something felt off; no, something felt wrong. The fragmented scenes no longer congealed in linear truth. I began to think aloud.

"In the woods, when Lance and I were together, he knew that David was coming to find me, that David would see us. Before David walked on the scene, before I had succumbed to Lance's touch, Lance told me that he already had known that I was pregnant, and that it excited him. But could he really have known without someone telling him? And who knew except Ruth? Why would she tell him my secret?"

As I began to detect my fall into deception, I raised my voice in an attempt to defend my foolish actions.

"Hadassah, Lance told me that he loved me, and that he wanted to take care of me and my unborn child. Can you understand how good that sounded? To have someone promise to protect me, only me, in this time of death? I wanted that. I was desperate for it, and so I said yes." I repeated the words slowly, "I said yes. And then I left with him. I left David. I left Jack. I left them all."

I began to calm down. I spoke softly and slowly as I continued, "Almost at once, I knew that I had made a mistake. At first I slowed and hesitated, but Lance pressed me to move on. It wasn't much later when I was forced to stop. It was a force greater than me; it was death. I tripped and fell onto a dead body. It was Lance's sister Leah. She had been following us, and someone didn't approve. That someone shattered her skull."

"What?" I could tell that Hadassah was lost in the shock of this news.

"Sarah," but it was not Hadassah's voice that called out to me this time.

"Sarah," the raspy voice repeated.

I turned and looked at Lance. How long had he been awake? How much had he heard?

"Sarah," I heard a third time. "Leah was not my sister."

There was a knock at the door.

"Hadassah." It was Paul.

"Yes," she replied, still shaken from Lance's words, and mine.

"We're up for guard duty."

"Paul, I can't go right now. I need to stay with Sarah."

"No Hadassah," I said. "It's better that Lance and I speak alone."

"Are you sure?" she asked. "I can have someone take my place."

"No," I assured her. "It's better that you go."

Hadassah slowly rose from the bed and opened the door. I gave her a look assuring her that it was okay for her to leave me and Lance alone. And after the door closed, I looked directly at him. His face was turned toward me and I could see that he had been crying.

"Leah was not my sister," he repeated.

"Well then who was she?" I asked.

"Leah was my wife."

12

Lies

I thought I might fall off the bed and onto the floor. This news seemed so bizarre, caught me so off-guard, that I thought maybe I hadn't even heard him correctly.

"What do you mean she was your wife?"

"Leah was my wife, Sarah," he said as he roughly wiped tears from his face. "We hadn't been married long, just six months or so."

"Just six months or so..." I repeated as the news continued to slowly sink in.

"It was troubled from the start," he began. "It was crazy, impulsive I guess. She needed me. She was so troubled. I thought I could help her. I wanted to protect her."

Yes, I thought. *Like he wanted to help and protect me. Controlling the weak made him feel strong.* I looked over at him on the bed. He had lifted himself slightly as the cleansing of confession fed him with renewed strength.

"Shortly after our impulsive courthouse wedding," he continued, "I knew I was screwed. Leah was insanely jealous of my friends. She wanted to be with me all of the time. I couldn't live; I could barely breathe! And then it happened, the explosion I mean. She grew worse, much worse. Finally, she really did have me all to herself, yet I felt even more alone when I was with her. When I found all of you...I was so happy, so relieved. Can you understand that?"

I just continued to sit in silence for a while until it all registered. This man who told me that he loved me, who tried to make love to me, who left his sister; correction his WIFE, with strangers while he took off with me...this man was Lance! I now felt the anger of a bullet in me. I stood and began to pace the small room.

"Are you kidding me?" I yelled. "How could you have just left her? How could you have been with another woman...with me? How could you tell me that you loved me, that you wanted only me when you were married to her? My God Lance, you and I, we were together right in front of her! Do you realize how sick that was?" I thought back to that first night, by the fire, when Lance and I fell asleep holding hands. I remember awakening to Leah holding a rock over our heads.

"She was going to kill us! The morning with the rock, she was going to kill us both, wasn't she?"

Lance tried to get up, but was still way too weakened by his wound. "Sarah, I know how terrible this sounds..."

"How terrible it sounds?" I was yelling now. "Try how terrible it is! Lance, how could you have just left her there? How could you have left with me? I believed you! I believed that you loved me!"

"I do love you," he said.

"Your love is sick! You are a liar and I am a fool."

"No!" He yelled as he grimaced with pain. "It's not a lie, and you are certainly not a fool!" He sank back down onto the bed as if the words agitated his injury. "Sarah, I didn't know how to take care of her. And Ruth, she wanted to. She was good with her. I thought Leah would be better off with her."

"But then, why not tell us the truth? Why not tell us that Leah was your wife?"

"Because we both know that it would never have been acceptable for me to leave her if you all knew the truth. Besides, there was you."

"What do you mean there was me?"

"When I saw you Sarah, I knew that I wanted to be with you. You were everything that Leah wasn't. You were confident, smart, rational. I wanted to be with you, and I knew that you would not even consider being with me if you knew the truth."

"Of course not!" I yelled. I felt so dirtied by lies and betrayal; it weakened me. I sat down on a corner of the bed and sank my head into my hands.

Lance struggled to rise to a seated position.

"Sarah," he whispered, "I'm sorry."

I thought back upon the last few months. I thought of Leah staring at me with distrust, Lance's aggressive advances, Claire's pushing of the relationship. I lifted my head from my hands and opened my eyes. There was more.

"What else?" I asked him.

"What do you mean?" He asked.

"What else haven't you told me? There's more, right?"

Lance eased himself against the back wall behind the bed. I remained on my small corner, as far from him as the little room would allow.

"Sarah, I didn't know you were pregnant until Claire told me. She overheard you talking with Ruth."

"Why would Claire tell you?"

"Look, I know this is going to sound really bad, but just try to understand, okay?"

I braced myself. "What is it?" I said calmly but with my teeth clenched.

"Claire wanted you gone. She saw how David looked at you; we all did. She wanted you to leave because you threatened all that she had, her life with David. At the same time, I wanted to free myself from Leah and spend the short remainder of my life with you. So, we made a deal. She would keep Leah with them, and I would take you away with me."

I turned and looked at him. I had not been prepared for this. "You traded me for her? You made a deal with our lives? What's wrong with you? Leah and I are not possessions, we are people, people with thoughts, feelings, souls...what were you thinking?"

"I was thinking that everyone could be happy, that everyone would get what they wanted. Claire could have David, Ruth could have Leah, and you and I could have each other. You said okay, you said you wanted to go with me. How is that different now?"

"Because it was all a lie! It was a set-up! That last night, when David found us, you set that all up didn't you? You set that up with Claire!"

His silence told me everything.

"Lance," I said through my anger, "How could you? How could you have been so cruel?"

He turned his face downward as he replied. "I'm sorry," he said. "I am so sorry. I just wanted you. I just wanted you is all."

"Now I get why Leah was following us," I said. "And now she's dead. Why? Why would someone kill her?"

Lance looked up and met my eyes. He spoke quietly, as if he was afraid someone else would hear. "I know who killed her," he said.

"Who?" I asked.

"You don't know her Sarah. You don't see it. That's another reason why I had to get you away."

I took in his words. "You mean Claire?" I asked.

"She didn't want to break our deal. She didn't want to risk you coming back."

"Wait a minute," I said. You think Claire killed Leah?"

"I don't think she did," he said. "I know she did."

Could this be true? If it was, then who else could get in Claire's way? Who else might she kill?

"My God, Lance! We have to find them! We need to warn the others!"

"No Sarah. If we go back, you're dead. I meant what I said. I intend to protect you always."

"I don't need your protection anymore," I said. And I meant it. I was no longer the weak girl who fed his need to feel strong. I didn't need anyone's protection. I was strong. I was on my own.

And just as I spoke the door burst open. It was Marcus.

"Sarah!" He shouted while handing me my two guns. "We're under attack. It's the corpses. They're trying to break into the house and steal everything, capture us; we need you!" Lance tried to rise from his seated position on the bed.

"You stay here," I commanded him. And then I took off, running behind Marcus through the kitchen and into a small room with the hidden hatch. I followed him through the secret door and into the sounds of shots and the smell of death.

13

Mt. Elbert

I followed Marcus around the left side of the house. In the distance I could see flashes as shots fired out toward the far right side. Then, all was silent. We crouched down behind what I supposed was once a small stone garden wall. Eva was there waiting for us. With her hand, she signaled that three were on the right side of the house and one on the left. It was crazy, I felt like I was in some WWII movie but with better acting. I closed my eyes to listen carefully to the shots. Remembering how I had used my hearing to target the shooter of Lance, I again allowed my senses to navigate this threat. I was careful not to refer to 'it' as a *he* or *she.* It was nothing more than a corpse. I had to remember that. It had chosen to give itself away. And when I was confident of its position and with my right arm outstretched toward it, I slowly rose to a standing position.

J.E.Byrne

"What are you doing?" whispered Marcus in a panic.

Eva turned around and then looked up as she realized my movement. She shook her head, warning me not to expose myself, but I felt transcendent. I squeezed my eyes and focused on the position. I knew I had it. I knew I could get it. And so I fired. One single shot at my target. We waited. One second, two, three...then we heard the sound of a body as it fell hard onto the ground. And then it began. Shots from the right began to rain on us. We could either fight back or run.

"Hadassah, Paul, and Mitch are out there," Eva shouted.

"Let's go," I said. Marcus agreed, and so the three of us ran out from behind our shelter with weapons drawn and shots firing. Suddenly, everything shifted into slow motion, sounds became muffled; flashes became multi-dimensional. Adrenaline fueled me as I ran toward the shots. I had a gun in each hand, and I imagined myself gracefully avoiding bullets like in the movies, as I confidently fired shots from both hands. I almost felt like I was moving underwater. I was in the zone, the killing zone, and I couldn't escape until I felt arms around me guiding me towards the ground. It was Marcus.

"Sarah," he said. "Sarah, it's over. You can stop." I looked at him and nodded, not sure I understood, but confident that I could trust him to let go of the mission. I realized that there weren't even any bullets left in my guns, that I had been firing empty shots. Then suddenly the chasm cracked and I was back. Back to real time, real sounds, and a visual of Hadassah weeping over a body. I ran over and knelt beside her. It was Paul.

The others from our group soon joined us. Eva and Marcus remained standing, holding each other's hands as if it could protect them from ever being separated by death. Mitch was studiously inspecting Paul, trying to remain an unaffected professional, looking to ensure that there still wasn't some way he could save him. After a few moments, his eyes met Hadassah's. And perhaps for the first time since Kelly's death, he spoke as a reborn leader. "Let's get him inside," he said.

Wordless and somewhat emotionless, we each bent down to carry a part of Paul's body, back toward the house and through the secret entrance. We entered the safe house and lay his body on the sofa.

"They got him." Hadassah whispered as she laid her head on Paul's chest.

"No Hadassah," Mitch quietly said, "They didn't. We'll bury him here, in this house, in a place where no one will ever find him." I knew the prevention. We didn't want anyone to cannibalize his body. I couldn't believe we had to think about such things now.

"I'm ready," she said. "Let's do it now."

In a way, this was a comfort; almost like we could recover from yet another loss if we could quickly file it away. We all laid our weapons on the table in the back of the room and then returned to stand near Hadassah to lift Paul to eternal safety.

"Do you want to say anything?" Mitch asked her.

"No," she said.

With free hands, we each held a part of Paul and slowly began to raise him. As we were preoccupied with our anticipated burial, we heard a sound come from the side entrance of the house. Looking up, I saw a stranger enter and raise his rifle. I met his eyes. He was one of them. He had survived the shooting and followed us through our secret portal. We were unarmed. We were dead.

A loud shout rang out as I closed my eyes and prepared for it. I didn't feel any pain. Is this what it was like? I slowly opened my eyes expecting to see angels or demons or something extraterrestrial, but instead I saw Lance standing with a smoking gun. As I watched his weakened body fall to the ground, I realized that he had saved my life, all of our lives, with his sacrifice.

The five of us remained standing in position. Everything had happened so fast that we didn't have time to react physically or emotionally. Finally, someone spoke. It was Eva. "He saved us."

We quickly lay Paul back onto the sofa and in the care of Hadassah. Mitch and I ran to where Lance had fallen, while Marcus and Eva went to make sure the intruder was dead; he was. Lance, on the other hand, was still very much alive.

"I'm okay," he whispered. "Just weak."

"Were you shot?" I asked.

"Not a chance," he stated.

Mitch gave him a quick check to be sure there were no new wounds. He nodded to me in affirmation. "He's just weak from the initial blood loss and infection."

I watched as Eva and Marcus re-armed themselves and then carried the corpse out of the house and hopefully far away into the woods, where he could become a victim of his own sin. Then, I looked over at Hadassah, who was whispering to Paul. I looked up at Mitch who had given life a second chance in his call to leadership. "I'll stay with Lance," I told him.

I watched him walk away to comfort his friend, while I stayed to comfort mine. Lance had me so confused; he had loved me, deceived me, and saved me all within the short confines of an apocalypse. I really didn't know if I should love him or hate him.

"Sarah," he said.

I just looked at him. I still didn't have the emotional ability to respond.

"Sarah," he continued. "You should go. Go find David. I know that you love him. And he loves you. Be strong. Watch out for Claire."

I met his eyes in silence. "What about you?" I managed to say.

"I'll be okay. I'm a quick healer," he said with a smile. "I still want to go south; I really need to work on my tan." I couldn't help but to give him a small smile back.

Marcus and Eva walked over to us and heard his last comment. "We're heading south," Eva said to him. "You can come with us."

"I'll go too," Mitch added as he walked over to join us. He looked at me when he spoke, "I'll make sure Lance gets the medical care he needs. You can go." Hadassah must have told him everything.

"I'm going with *you* Sarah," Hadassah said from afar. "I'm going with you to Mt. Elbert."

I looked up, not at all surprised that my destination had been revealed to her. The supernatural no longer shocked me; it had become a part of me. I nodded to them all. My decision was made. I was leaving with Hadassah. I was going to find David...and maybe even Mt. Elbert.

14

Journey

The next days were filled with a mix of sadness and vigor. While we each prepared for our newly designed futures; we boarded, nailed shut, and heavily guarded our one gateway to the outside world. We knew that the next time it released us, we would never return. The safe house was a time of rest, a short chapter in an ongoing novel of survival and struggle. Hadassah, while focused on our preparations, tasked in the silence of private grief as she mourned her loss of Paul. We had buried him in a secret place high within the attic of the house. No one would ever find him there; no one would ever be able to adulterate our last images of him. It felt right that he was buried within the heights of the house, that he would be as close to the heavens as we could deliver him.

We spent our days and nights in planning. We combed through all of the supplies the group had collected over the past weeks: bullets, dried cereal, pet food, applesauce, peanut butter, hand sanitizer, various medicines, candles and matches; these were just some of the treasures for which the attackers had been willing to kill and die. Eva and Marcus worked to divide everything so that we could all have some time of sustenance until we could replenish. On Hadassah's urging, I shared my secret with them, which entitled me to a bit more food than I deserved, but I gladly accepted.

I shared my maps with everyone. Under the light of the gas lantern, we poured over which routes to take to our various destinations. Hadassah and I decided that we would try to follow a direct path following Castleman Run Road to route 70. The map revealed it as a seven mile trek, so even though it covered some rustic terrain, we figured we could make it within the confines of one day. The others were also going to travel that path, but planning to leave a few days later than we, after they were sure that Lance could make the journey. But once Hadassah and I hit 70, we were turning right, while the rest of them would make a left.

Lance's strength continued to improve. I barely slept ever since my journey had been reignited, and when I did, it was nowhere near the room where he and I once lay together. When he joined the group in the main room, he and I never spoke; Lance likely felt shame and I felt confusion. I hated him for his deceit, and yet recognized that he had twice saved my life, and perhaps somewhat merited forgiveness for his confession and my release. But then again, I wasn't a product. I shouldn't have had to been set free. But it was I who ignored a freedom that I always had; I had just been blind. And now, three days after my decision to leave, I could see.

"Ready?" I asked Hadassah.

She nodded in affirmation, still seemingly too mournful to speak.

I inspected my belongings. I had two newly reloaded guns, six filled water bottles, one half-filled jar of peanut butter, two containers of applesauce, two cans of cat food (it truly tasted the same as tuna), three candles with two boxes of matches, a lighter, two boxes of bullets, two bottles of hand sanitizer, and an almost full box of Lucky Charms. I could have taken the Cheerios; I actually preferred them, but figured I'd side with luck. And in case luck ran out, I had a butcher knife tucked inside of my left sock and a gun inside of each coat pocket. I rolled up my sleeping bag and placed it on the tail of my backpack holder. I was ready.

"Be careful out there Sarah," Eva said.

Strangely, my eyes filled with tears as I backed up and met her eyes. She was the type of person who carefully chose to whom she gave her trust – and she had given hers to me. She was hard, but real, and I respected that. I mourned the loss, knowing that our paths would probably not cross again. I took a great risk in vulnerability, but I didn't care; I gave her a hug. At first, unused to such affections, she froze; but eventually warmed under my embrace and wrapped her small, yet strong arms around my shoulders.

"Bye," she said. I released her.

Touched by my show of affection, Marcus followed by giving me a quick and somewhat awkward hug. But I appreciated the gesture.

"Take good care of one another," I said. They held hands, gave me one last look, and then turned away to continue prepping for their own journey. I turned toward the opposite direction to watch Hadassah and Mitch preparing her for our departure. And then I went to see Lance. I felt compelled to make one last visit to the room where he had taken his refuge.

I slowly opened the door. It creaked, yet he remained still, his body illuminated in the candlelight, turned away from me and toward the wall. I felt relieved. I wasn't sure if I really wanted to see him; I wasn't sure if he deserved a goodbye. But as I turned away, he spoke:

"Sarah," I heard his voice, once so familiar to me.

He turned over to meet my gaze. He looked so much better. The color had returned to his face and he moved seemingly free from discomfort. I just stood staring at him; I couldn't bring myself to speak. I watched as he sat up and then moved closer to me.

He held out his hand. Inside of its palm lay my cell phone, the one I had given him back when we were still with the others, the one that had once magically turned on to reveal the time before returning to its dark tomb. I reached out and took it from his hand. I stared at its familiar shape. There was a time when this device was my lifeline; until now I had forgotten all about it.

"I want you to have it, just in case."

"Thanks." It was all I could say. I turned to walk away.

"You can do it," he said.

I turned around and looked at him. "Do what?" I asked.

"You can survive. You can make it to Mt. Elbert."

"I thought you didn't believe in visions," I said.

"I believe in you," he answered back.

I looked at him one last time, slowly and deliberately, knowing that as soon as I walked out of the room, he would be gone from my life.

"Bye, Lance," I said.

"Bye, Sarah."

Before I walked out of the door, I pulled his revolver out of my pocket and sat it on the table next to the bed. Then I turned and walked out of the door, briefly flashing back to memories of flirting with him by the fire, and eating valuable junk food while kissing in a mildewed barn. He had committed some terrible sins, but so had I, and he had given me some moments of reprieve. For a brief moment I thought I could one day forgive him, and then my thoughts were shifted as I saw Hadassah, backpack on, waiting for me as I re-entered the main room. I nodded at her, picked up my things and walked over to the safe house exit. Mitch walked toward Hadassah.

"You sure you don't want me to go with you?" he said softly by Hadassah's side.

"No," she replied. "This is my path – not yours."

Mitch nodded and then kissed her on the cheek, releasing Hadassah to me. He then took a sledge hammer and pried open the small door to the outside. Bending down I felt the cold air rush to greet me. I was back. I was on with my journey, and this time I was the captain. Hadassah followed me through the door and as we walked away; we heard the sounds of nails being forced through walls, sealing any feelings of regret.

We walked for about a half mile before we reached a main road, which my map identified as Castleman Run. Making a sharp left, we set off on our course heading toward route 70. The air was chilly, but dry, and the sky remained lifeless and dark. I was able to clearly see Hadassah at my side, and the shadows of tree skeletons and their shredded debris along the sides of the road. Hope's kicks tickled my insides and reminded me of my will to live.

"You okay?" I asked Hadassah.

"Yeah," she responded.

"I know what it's like to lose someone you love," I said.

"How did you get through it?" she asked.

"I didn't," I confessed. I thought back to losing the man I had loved most in the world, my father. "When my dad died, I chose to never face the pain in its reality. I just went on with life as if it never happened, and I hurt myself and others along the way. So I guess what I'm saying is not only did I not handle it well, I didn't handle it at all."

"So that didn't work for you?" she asked. "Just avoiding the hurt?"

"No. I've come to recognize it as my biggest failure in my pre-apocalyptic life."

"So are you suggesting that it's okay for me to feel miserable?" she asked.

"Yes," I said. "It's better to deal with your emotions now rather than wait for them to resurface at some inconvenient time in the future."

"You mean if there is a future," she said.

"Yeah, if there is one," I agreed.

"Sarah?" she asked.

"Yeah?"

"Is it okay if we stop for few minutes?" I watched as she walked toward the side of the road.

"Sure," I said, although I felt slightly inconvenienced at the thought of delay. And then words once again came to me: "Rejoice with those who rejoice; weep with those who weep." I was suddenly filled with an empathy and tenderness that was new to me. It filled me. And then I watched Hadassah collapse onto the bare ground, put her head into her hands and begin to weep. I walked over to her and lowered myself to the ground. I gently lay my right arm around her shoulders; I felt her pain and she felt mine. Together we cried tears of mourning; she for her lover, and me for my father, as I finally let go of this man who had died years before. When it was over, we stood up, gave each other a nod, and continued walking along the road.

15

Hadassah

After a day's walk, our feet touched the crossroads of what our map told us were Castleman Run Road and Route 70.

"We did it," I said. "We're here." As I spoke a chilly rain began to fall; its black streaks a reminder of the many challenges that lay ahead.

"Let's find some shelter," Hadassah suggested.

We walked on for about a mile until we saw shadows from a small cluster of buildings. Aware of the dangers that prowled in such places, we kept silent and alert, continuing to walk past the main structures and toward a large sign. Not wanting to attract strangers to our presence, I did not ignite my lighter, but instead chose to remain in the dark, waiting to read the sign until we came almost directly upon it.

"Welcome to West Virginia, Wild and Wonderful," I read out loud.

"Sounds like an adventure," Hadassah answered.

We kept walking, past the sign, past the rest stop. We found an outside picnic area with a covering. Quickly we walked over to accept its shelter. We sat underneath of a large table, sitting close to each other for both warmth and protection.

"Should we go in and check for food?" she asked.

"Yes, we definitely should," I replied. "But first, let's rest. I'm exhausted."

Hadassah agreed. We placed Hadassah's sleeping bag on top of the cement floor and each collapsed onto it. Next we laid my bag on top of our chilled bodies.

"This is the life," I said.

"No not yet." She placed a can of Little Friskies in my hand. "Now it's the life," she added.

"No not yet," I said. I pulled out my box of Lucky Charms and sat it between us. "Paradise." I smiled at her.

"Yeah, more like Paradise Lost," she answered.

I laughed at the allusion that was truth. We allowed ourselves to eat until we were full, and then we lay back to rest our weary bodies and souls. I'm not sure how long I slept, maybe a few hours. When I awoke, I took a deep breath and gently placed my hands on Hope. She was quiet as if the quirky meal and rest prepared her for a long nap. I closed my eyes and thought about David. I remembered the time when we were first alone. It was after we had explored the abandoned school and found nothing but death. I was afraid and defeated and chose to isolate myself by establishing my personal space away from the group. David had found me. It was the night he confessed that he had dreamed of me even before our first meeting. It was also the night when I realized through this confession that I, too, had dreamed of him before we met. The connection was overpowering; it felt almost supernatural, and I remember that at that moment, I had felt a type of attraction that I had never known, and perhaps would never know again. It was deep and rich and had nothing to do with sex or appearances. I wanted to feel it again. Real love. True love. I heard Hadassah awaken with a deep sigh.

"Hadassah," I said. "Tell me about Paul."

Hadassah took a few moments to gather her thoughts. I hoped that I hadn't overstepped my boundaries into her private thoughts. Just as I was about to tell her that she didn't have to answer, she began talking.

"I was married before," she said.

"You mean not to Paul?" I asked.

"Yes, not to Paul. I was married for almost two years before the explosion. My husband was an operating room nurse. He was on the fifth floor of the hospital…you know…when it happened."

"Did you try to find him?"

"Yes. But of course I couldn't; he didn't…"

"I know," I said.

"It was before I gave up, before I chose to end my life. Before Paul found me."

"Did you love him too? Your husband, I mean?"

"In a way I did. We had a good relationship. We were friends and we liked and respected one another. It was an amicable love."

"But it was different with Paul?" I asked.

"Yes, it was exponentially different. With Paul, even in our short time together, there was a deeper connection. It was more than friendship, it was more than attraction; it was almost mystical. It was like we knew each other's souls. I guess that sounds pretty lame, doesn't it?"

"No," I said. "I think it sounds beautiful."

"Yeah," she continued. "It was beautiful, so much so that I knew it couldn't last. It was too precious, too vulnerable, like a fragile piece of crystal or the last remaining animal in a species. My love for him was so deep, it almost hurt me sometimes."

Her words punctured me. That was how I felt when I thought about David. My feelings were so intense that they hurt. I longed for him. I ached for him.

"Does this describe how you feel about David?" she asked me.

"Yes," I confessed.

"Then we'll find him Sarah. We won't stop until we find him."

"Thanks," I said. But I wasn't sure if we ever would. I thought about what she had said, that love like that was almost too precious to survive. I couldn't think about him anymore. It was all too much.

"Lance was in love with you," she said. "I could see it in his eyes."

"He lied to me," I said.

"What happened?" she asked.

"He tricked me into leaving with him. He promised someone else, Claire, that he would take me away from David, so that she could have him, so that David wouldn't leave her for me."

"And then Lance would get you," she said. "It's deceitful, but it does make sense."

"Maybe," I said, "but it's even more deceitful than that. Claire promised to keep his sister Leah with them if he took me away."

"But Leah wasn't his sister, right?" Hadassah asked.

"Yes, that was another lie," I said. "Leah was his wife."

"Wow. So he made a deal with Claire," she said.

"He made a deal with the devil," I added.

"But he lost in the end, didn't he?" she remarked.

"We all lost in the end," I said.

"You haven't lost yet," she answered. "One of us has to end up at Mt. Elbert. One of us has to survive, and it has to be you."

"Why does it have to me?" I laughed.

"Because there are three of you counting on it."

I sat up and looked at her. She was right, there were three.

"Ready to go find some food?" I asked.

"Yeah," she replied. "I'm ready."

We packed up our things and planned our reconnaissance mission for the West Virginia rest stop. I wondered if inside I'd find another young family like the Eirmanns or perhaps even a wise, old couple like Jonathan and Elizabeth. Maybe I'd find more danger, or possibly even death. Increasingly hardened in such realities, I led the way toward the sign that promised "Wild and Wonderful." And just as I was about to open the door, I felt a strange buzzing in my pocket. I reached my hand inside and pulled out my phone. It was powered on, and there was a text.

16

Wild and Wonderful

The light of the phone illuminated its presence. I looked down at it in shock before my mind registered that I needed to quickly read before its power was again removed. *must find. head to wheeling. d*

"Sarah," Hadassah breathlessly said, "is that your phone?"

"Yes," I said. My hands were trembling as they looked again at the resurrected phone. "Hadassah," I added, "it's Tuesday. It's 4:05 pm on Tuesday, September 16th." Knowing this gave me such a feeling of empowerment, such a feeling of control. Hope gave me a strong kick on the right side of my belly. And then the phone went dark.

"What did it say? Who was it from?"

I looked up at her. "I think it was from David," I said.

"Oh my God Sarah, what did he say?"

"The message said to head to Wheeling. It said 'must find.' It was signed d.

"D? Do you know any other D's besides David who might be alive? Who might have your phone number?"

I paused because the answer was no; I hadn't met any other post-apocalyptic D's, but also because I didn't even remember ever giving David my phone number. Yet I knew, deep down I *knew* that it was David...that the message was from him.

"It was him," I confidently told her.

"Well then let's go," she said. "Let's head to Wheeling. I know the way."

I had forgotten that Hadassah had worked in Wheeling. It hadn't been so long ago when she had left there with Paul.

"We can take route 70 to route 2," she said as she walked toward me. "I think it's only about fifteen or twenty miles from the state border. We can get there in a few days."

"Are you sure you're ready to go back?" I asked her. This was the place where she had witnessed a hospital of lost lives. This was the place where she had almost lost her own.

"Yes, I'm ready. Reuniting you with David gives meaning to Paul's words, that we, that I survived for something greater. I want to help you do this. I want to live Paul's promise."

I still held my hand on the slimy glass of the rest stop door. I think I may have been in shock. If I truly believed this message, and that it was from David, it meant that not only was he alive, but he was looking for me, and he was only a day or two away. I wanted to sprint ahead to Wheeling. I wanted to jump into his arms. I wanted to tell him that I loved him. But something was stopping me. It was either common sense, or the Darwinian gift of survival instinct that I was gaining with each day of life in an apocalypse.

"Sarah, what's wrong?" Hadassah asked as she walked toward me.

"I'm scared to have hope. I'm scared that it will be taken away."

"Nothing is going to take this away. We're going to make it. You're going to find him. We can do this Sarah. We will do this. Now come on, let's go. First, we can check the rest stop for food, and then we can start walking."

Invigorated, I stood and accepted our newly mapped-out odyssey. I only hoped that the gods and goddesses didn't intervene and delay me twenty years. I was pretty confident we didn't have anywhere close to twenty more years anyway.

I reached into my pocket and pulled out my newly loaded gun. Next to me, Hadassah held the hunting rifle I had taken from the corpse. I looked over at her. Slowly I cracked open the front door just wide enough for her to sneak through, the hunting rifle leading the way. She crept over to the left wall, I to the right. It was dark and silent and we both remained still, waiting for others, if there were others, to make the first sound. But there was nothing. We waited and waited, and there was nothing.

Finally, I flicked on my lighter. In its glow I saw only the remains of what once was. Charred corpses, overturned tables, broken glass and items thrown all over the large tiled floor. Whatever had been here had long been destroyed. It was just another reminder of how in survival, we were losing what made us human, what separated us from the animals. I saw Hadassah walking toward me. We each just stood still, taking in the destruction.

"Let's stay together," I said. She nodded as we slowly made our way around the ruins: a TCBY, a Sbarro, a Burger King...everything emptied, everything dead. Out of the corner of my right eye I saw a Starbucks. I remembered the last time I was in one; it was with Lance. It was when I first fell in lust with him, certainly not in love, but admittedly in lust. I wondered if he had yet left the safe house. I wondered if he was okay. I should have told him that I forgave him, even before I actually did. I should have at least given him that. Now, walking around, looking at the remnants of sin, I really did forgive him. I forgave us. We were all living in a time that fortified poor judgment. We were all guilty of many things.

"Sarah, listen!" Hadassah whispered to me. We both froze.

"I don't hear anything," I whispered back. We waited a few more minutes before Hadassah shrugged off what I assumed was her imagination.

I picked up some discarded napkins and stuffed them in my pack. Hadassah scored some ketchup and relish packets; they could hopefully provide some type of vegetable supplement. We gleaned some plastic forks and some packets of salt. Confident that we had found the very last treasures, we made ready to exit. As we passed by the rest rooms, I had to stop. Who knew when we would next have the opportunity to use real bathrooms and running water? Who knew when whatever built up pressure was powering the water system would run out? While Hadassah stood on guard, I smothered my hair and face with soap and rinsed again and again in the sink. I looked in the mirror and wondered what David would see. For the first time, I thought I looked strong.

"You finished in there beauty queen?" Hadassah yelled in.

"Yes," I said as I walked out to relieve her of guard duty.

"Wow, you really do look refreshed," she said. "David will be impressed."

"Your turn," I said ignoring her teasing.

I watched as Hadassah entered our rest stop oasis. Outside of the rest room, I stood up against the wall with my hands in my pockets, ready to grab a weapon if needed. I could hear her humming a tune, its melody echoing against the walls. I allowed myself to let my guard down, as it was pretty obvious that no one had visited this rest stop in a long time. For a second I closed my eyes. I thought back to the night when Jack and I had returned to my home. It was after the explosion, after I had found the charred remains of my mom and Ben. I remembered jumping into a cold shower and scrubbing myself until my skin was raw. It was as though I could remove the pain, but of course I couldn't then, just as I couldn't now. I opened my eyes to meet the darkness. I saw movement.

I grabbed my gun and aimed it ahead. The movement was gone. I crept down low and along the belly of the floor. I knew that I had seen something. As I approached the doors to the outside, I again saw the moving shadow. Illuminated by the outside haze, the shadow came into view and I saw that it was a rat. A very large rat. I screamed.

"Sarah!" Hadassah ran out of the bathroom with her rifle at the ready.

"Over here," I called. "I'm okay."

As she approached me she said, "What happened?" She was out of breath from panic.

"Sorry," I said. "It was a rat."

"Where?" she asked.

"It ran out of the door, through a hole in the broken glass."

"Gross," she said.

I agreed. I hated rats, rodents of any kind that is. I didn't even like squirrels. But then, I rationalized, *rats meant food!*

"Hadassah, if there was a rat, and a fat one at that, there must be food in here somewhere!" I looked at the path from which the rat had travelled. I began to follow it, with Hadassah close behind me. It led us down a back hallway with several doors on each side. I flicked on my lighter. The doors were labeled with custodial titles that didn't look promising. And then we saw another rat. It was scurrying from a door on the left. Could someone have hidden food in there? Could someone still be in there? I looked at Hadassah. We nodded in tacit agreement. I stood on one side of the door, she on the other, our weapons drawn. With my free hand, I slowly opened the door. And out poured what seemed like legions of rats. Big, ugly, hairy, fat rats. I screamed and took off for the main dining area, Hadassah at my heels. We jumped on top of a table watching the rats in panic, running in all directions. It was disgusting and I was totally freaked. I hate rats.

Hadassah and I stayed on the table unsure of what to do. It could be hours, even days before the disgusting carnivores disappeared. Some started to crawl up on the table. We tried to kick them away with our feet. More got up on the table with us. I remembered learning about the corpse rats in the trenches during WWI. I was beginning to panic. Rats were beginning to crawl around my feet. They were biting and clawing at my legs.

"We've got to get out of here!" Hadassah screamed.

I lifted my gun and shot at the floor. As rat guts splattered everywhere along the tile, surviving rats parted like the sea. I shot again and again to make a rat free trail. I jumped to the floor, panicked and running as fast as I could; out of the room, out of the door and not stopping until I was free of the disgusting corpse eaters. Hadassah jumped up next to me and onto the picnic table where we had before found shelter. We were both panicked and out of breath. I lifted up my pants and inspected my legs. The area around my ankles was littered with the graffiti of scratches painted with my blood. I looked at Hadassah as she revealed the same disturbing artwork. We reached into our backpacks and pulled out bottles of hand sanitizer, smearing the red paint and destroying its destruction; I welcomed the burn. I hated rats. I really hated them.

After we calmed down and our breathing slowed, Hadassah spoke. "Even after all we've been through," she said, "all of the living and all of the dying; that was incredibly terrifying."

I agreed, but then realized one very important thing that we had overlooked in our terror. I turned to Hadassah and shared my epiphany.

"Hadassah," I said. "The animals, they're back."

"Yeah, and apparently they're even hungrier than we are," she added.

"Wonder what unfortunate thing or things were in the storage room," I said.

She just shook her head and said, "Let's get out of here."

We began walking as far away from Wild and Wonderful as our tired legs could carry. And as we walked, I thought to myself that small predators were just as lethal as the large. I slipped my right hand into my pocket, reaping comfort in my metal companion.

17

Villains

We each walked in the silence of our memories. I thought about my parents, my brother, my friends, and even all of smaller things I loved like movies and chocolaty brownies, following television series and running outside on sunny days while listening to my iPod. I thought about school, and reading good books, crowded hallways, and flirting, and even lip-gloss for my forever chapped lips. Earth, you really are too wonderful for anyone to realize you. Thorton Wilder was right. I had taken everything for granted.

"Hadassah," I said, interrupting the silence and surely her private thoughts, "I'm tired. Let's stop for the night."

She agreed.

We walked off of the highway and into the empty trees and bushes that hopefully would keep us safe and hidden for the night. Although we had passed some buildings along the way, after our rat adventure, we wanted to stay far away from carnivorous draws. After about a half-mile or so, we both somehow knew it was time to stop. I pulled my backpack off and lay it on the ground. I smiled to myself recognizing that years of carrying heavy schoolbooks on my back had proved valuable after all. Next I lay my sleeping bag on the ground and plopped myself on the top. I rolled up my pant legs and checked my wounds from the rats. The blood had dried inside of the scratches, and now they just looked like little lines of red pen scribbled around my ankles. After lowering my pants, I pulled out a water bottle and took a long, deep drink.

"I'm starving," Hadassah said to my side. I smiled at her as she pulled out a partially eaten jar of peanut butter and a plastic spoon. She unscrewed the lid and dipped in her ladle, filling her mouth with a huge blob. I thought I'd lighten the mood by at that precise moment asking her to talk.

"Hadassah," I asked, "tell me a story. And be sure to fit in how you got such a fancy name."

She tried to open her mouth, but it was glued shut with her dinner. We both laughed.

"How about I check out our destination on the map while you swallow your kid paste," I said.

She nodded and then mumbled, "Good idea."

I pulled out my road map and lay it on the ground. I lit one of my candles and set it to the side. I ran my finger along route 70. Considering the location of Castleman Run Road, the rest stop, and the miles we had walked since, I figured we were still about eleven miles from Wheeling. I grabbed a pencil from the front of my pack. I drew a calendar on the back. My phone had revealed the date and time as September 16, 4:05 p.m. Feeling confident we had survived another day, I drew a large X through September 16. I stared at the promise of September 17. This could be the day that I was reunited with David. This could be the day that Hope and I could fall into his arms. Hope. I did some calculating in my mind. I was roughly five months pregnant. I lay back, one hand resting on Hope, the other still on the map.

"We're so close," Hadassah said to my side.

"Yeah," I added, "so close and yet so far."

"Sounds like lame music lyrics."

"I actually think they were," I said.

"Sarah, you better eat something."

"Yes mom."

"Hey, I have two of you to keep safe and healthy until I can release you into the care of another."

"Release me? You're not going to release me; you're gonna come with me to Mt. Elbert, remember?"

"Mt. Elbert," she whispered. "I had forgotten about that."

"How did you know?" I asked her. "How did you know that was where I was going?"

"It's hard to explain," she said. The words just kind of came to me. In an instant, I thought, no, I knew that Mt. Elbert was your destination."

"And yours too, right?"

"Right," she said. But she didn't say it with conviction that I sought.

"I've been there before," she said.

"You have?" I perked up with great interest. "What's it like? When were you there?"

"I was there as a kid," she answered. "My Aunt and Uncle took me to Colorado to visit some distant relatives. While we were there, my Uncle and I attempted some mountain climbing. We were told that Mt. Elbert was a good 'first climb' experience, so we ventured there."

"What did it look like?" I asked. I was pretty sure it wouldn't have been showcased with rainbows and jewels like I had seen in my dream, but I just wanted to be sure.

"It was beautiful," she said. "We didn't make it the whole way to the summit; I was only ten or eleven and the trail got pretty steep after a while. But still, I remember the pine trees, the rocky path, and other travelers cheering each other on."

"When I dream of it," I said, "it is covered in bright jewels and has walls of gleaming precious metals."

"Well I only saw Mt. Elbert for real, a very long time ago, and in its natural, earthly state. I haven't had any of your ethereal dreams."

"It happens to me all of the time," I said.

"What does?" she asked.

"The strange words...thoughts, dreams, and visions. Ever since the explosion, it's like there is someone who keeps sending me secret messages. Sometimes I think maybe it's God. Is that weird?"

"No," she said. "It's not weird at all. I think it is God," she added.

"Why?" I asked. "I mean, if God did exist, why would He have let this happen? Why wouldn't He have protected us...all of us? Why would He have allowed some of us to live and not others? Why would He be helping me now? I'm a horrible person; I've done some horrible things. I don't deserve life or help."

"Sarah," she said in a soft voice, "first of all, we have *all* done horrible things, not just to survive, but also before. The truth is that none of us deserves life or help."

"Then why did some of us get it, and some of us not? It's not fair is it?"

"No it's not fair," she said turning away, probably thinking of all her losses. "And I always hate when people say that 'life isn't fair.' It sounds like a cop out, and I'm not going to pretend to have answers for the big questions that elude me. All I do know is that for some reason, we were created with the ability to make choices, both good and bad, and we have control over that; likewise, we were created to both live and die, and for some reason we don't have control over that. I mean look at us, are you really glad that you survived the explosion? Do you think it's *lucky* that you get to still live amidst all of this? I tried to leave. I tried to kill myself, but as you recall, I was denied that right. I was seemingly not allowed to die. I don't know the reasons for it all, and I'm not going to pretend that I do, but I do believe that our journey is a part of a bigger story."

"A bigger story," I repeated. Where had I heard this before? Jenna. Jenna told me that she believed in a bigger story.

"Why does there have to be a bigger story?" I asked. "Why can't our lives just be small, simple stories, with storybook childhoods, and fairytale romances that last forever?"

"Maybe that's how the big story ends." she said. "But maybe we need to experience the little ones in order to understand the gift of the larger one."

"It's all either too complicated or too simple," I said. I lay back on my sleeping bag and closed my eyes.

"Eat," she said as she again passed some food my way. Hope had been so quiet I had forgotten about her. I realized that she was a little story within my bigger one, and that my story needed to survive in order for hers to be written. I grabbed the half-eaten jar of peanut butter and the spoon and stuffed a mouthful between my lips.

"Hadassah," I said as I let the peanut butter melt inside of my mouth. "Tell me your story."

"It's nothing great," she replied.

"Well apparently it's vital to a bigger one, right?" She laughed as she, too, lay back on her portable bed.

"Maybe," she said.

"Come on," I pleaded, "it'll help me fall asleep."

"So you think I'm boring?"

"No," I laughed. "I think that your story will be so engaging that it will allow me to forget everything else."

"Okay, Sarah," I heard her say with a sigh.

"I'm not originally from West Virginia; I was actually born in Israel," she began, "and my name is just an old family name, by the way; nothing significant that I'm aware of. My parents were killed in a bombing when I was just a kid, so I was sent to America to live with my mom's brother, Ben, and his wife Ruth."

"Wait, wait, wait," I interrupted her. "What do you mean your parents were killed in a bombing? That's not just a passing comment Hadassah."

"Sorry, it's just that I don't know much about it; I was just a kid."

"Was it a terrorist bombing? How did you survive?" I asked.

"I wasn't with them and yes, it was a terrorist bombing. But you have to understand, in Israel, we were used to bombings. It wasn't like in America where everyone constantly walks around in fear, well, until now of course. Now, living in fear is part of what keeps us alive."

"Yeah," I said. "I'm sorry I interrupted, please continue."

"Okay, where was I?"

"You went to live with Ben and Ruth," I said.

"Yeah," she continued. "Ben and Ruth lived in Alexandria, Virginia, and had no kids of their own. Anyway, my uncle was incredibly protective of me, but not in a burdensome way; it was a kind and caring protection. My aunt and uncle were incredibly intelligent and each held pretty solid jobs, even though neither had been given the opportunity to go to college. They both worked at a hospital; my uncle was in human resources and my aunt, was a receptionist for the radiology unit. So, as you can imagine, their idea of a bigger story for me was that I would be able to go to college and further our family's vocational path. So I worked hard to please them, and in doing so, excelled at school. Eventually, I went through the nursing program at John Hopkins, and landed a job at Wheeling Hospital. That was four years ago. They were so proud of me, so excited to see my life, in their minds, exceed their own. What they didn't realize, however, is that it was their lives that allowed mine. They were amazing people."

"Did you see them after you moved?"

"Yes. I visited them frequently. It was my uncle who encouraged me to marry Kevin."

"He must have really liked him."

"Yeah, well Kevin was a great guy. He was kind and well-educated; he was older than I and Ben knew he could provide a good and safe home for me. I'm sure Ben hoped that Kevin and I would have many kids, allowing each to strive even further than we had.

"How so?"

"I don't know; maybe they'd become a doctor, or even find a cure for cancer or some other horrible disease."

"That would be great," I said thinking of my father.

"Yeah, it could have been," she said.

"Did you and Kevin plan on having kids?"

"I guess so; eventually we would have I think. I don't know, even though we got along fine, we never really had a romantic kind of love. Our relationship was more like one of esteemed colleagues."

"Ouch," I said.

"Not really," she replied. "I hadn't ever been in love; I didn't believe in it. I thought romantic love only happened in film, novels and TV. So, I didn't know what I was missing."

"Until you met Paul," I said.

"Yes, until I met Paul." She grew quiet.

"I'm sorry, Hadassah. I didn't mean to remind you of him."

"It's okay. I like to be reminded. I loved him deeply."

"Did you and Paul ever…were you both ever…um?"

"You want to know if we had sex?" she asked.

"Yeah, that's what I want to know," I confessed.

"Yes," she confessed. "Of course we did. I'm kind of an old-fashioned girl, so we shared some post-apocalyptic vows, and then, what can I say? It was wonderful; no, it was better than wonderful; it was body and spirit all coming together. It was all types of love coming together."

"Wow," was all I could say.

"So I guess you and David never…"

"No," I quickly said. "I've never been with anyone." I remembered my swollen belly and added, "Well except for when it was once forced upon me."

"Sarah, I'm so sorry," she said as she sat up and looked at me. "I'm so sorry that happened to you."

"Yeah," I replied. "But then again, it gave me Hope didn't it?"

"Yes it did," she said.

"Hadassah?"

"Yeah?"

"Do you think God's angry with us? Do you think that's why this happened?"

"I don't know," she said. "Maybe he's just trying to get our attention; he's certainly gotten mine."

Hadassah and I were quiet after that, each retreating into our own thoughts. I considered her words. If it was God who was sending me the strange messages, he certainly was trying to get my attention too, but for some reason I kept fighting him along the way. I wondered if I ignored him long enough, if he would leave me alone. I was pretty angry with him after all; I realized that I had been for a long time. I closed my eyes and tried to sleep, but it would not come. My mind was churning with thoughts of big and small stories, belief and unbelief, anger and forgiveness. It was a quintessential time of paradox and it left me tossing and turning, even after hearing the soft breathing of a sleeping Hadassah. After what seemed like hours, I gave up and walked off to try and resolve my inconsistencies. The air was its usual misty cold, but at least no rain was falling. The shadows told me that it was early morning, not quite the extreme black of the night. I felt Hope begin to move beneath my clothing, a reminder that I needed to return to camp and get something to eat. And just as I took my first steps back towards Hadassah, I heard a predatory growling noise.

I stopped and listened. Again I heard the sound. I turned my head, but couldn't see anything. I couldn't be more than 50 yards from where Hadassah was sleeping. How could I get back to her in warning? What if whatever was growling at me already found her? I slipped my hand into my pocket and slowly folded my hand around my gun. Then I lifted my loaded hand and took a step forward, away from the rustling in the woods that followed me. I turned, lifted my two hands and fired. First there was the wail of a wounded creature, then more sounds that were ignited with movement. Whatever they were, they were coming for me. I fired off one more shot, then with no other option, I took off running. I purposely ran away from Hadassah's location in an attempt to save her. I could feel the large presence of evil, and it was catching up to my shadow. Its growl grew to two or three as I realized I was being chased by a group. Of what, I wasn't sure. They caught up with me and I could feel their teeth pulling at me, my flesh being ripped from my body. Was this how it was going to end? Hope. I couldn't let them get her; her poetry was not yet written.

"Sarah! Over here!" It was Hadassah. How did she get to where I was running? I had purposefully run away from where she had been sleeping.

"Sarah, run!" she yelled as she raised her rifle and began to shoot at whatever was on my trail. I heard a mixture of wailing and savagery. The shots distracted the attackers. I slowed to look behind me. My predators were a pack of dogs. The surviving animals had resurfaced because like us, they were starving; and like many of us, they too had turned to barbarity. I watched as they turned from me and toward Hadassah and her weapon.

"Run, Sarah! Get out of here!" she yelled. "You've got to save Hope, find David! Run! Go! Now Sarah! Run!"

I didn't know what to do. I couldn't leave her here to die for me. And yet, as I stood there ignoring her command, I watched the surviving dogs jump on top of my friend and shred her to pieces. My mouth gaped open. I was frozen. And then I heard a voice again, but of course it was not Hadassah's this time.

"You need to run now!" it commanded. "Run to your left where you will find a shelter. Go inside and lock the door. Now Sarah. Now!" I could feel the speaker's breath on the nape of my neck. It was loud and forceful, and it demanded obedience. I ran as fast as I could to my left, where sure enough I saw a small wooden shack. I ran inside, shut the door, and slid the door's padlock across just as I heard clawing and scratching on the other side. I was safe. Hadassah was dead. And she had died for me.

18

The Shack

I fell to my knees and dragged my wounded body
across the small dirt floor as far away from the death eaters
as I could. Leaning against the small back wall I waited
while my breath calmed and my wounds throbbed. Finally
the predators, realizing that the door would not give,
relented and silence ensued. I was alone. I was safe. I was
safe for now. As shock ebbed, I snapped to the reality of my
injuries. I thrust my hands under my clothing and on top of
Hope. While my abdomen was uninjured, blood seeped
from the right side of my pants. Slowly, I pulled the fabric
down, over my hips and down my long legs until my pants
sat on top of the heaviness of my muddied boots. There was
blood everywhere, too much to determine the source. I
grabbed my backpack and unzipped its core. I pulled out
one of my water bottles and first took a long, hard swig, and

then poured the rest on top of my bloody right leg. I could see two deep puncture wounds on my thigh and as quickly as I poured water to wash away the blood, it refilled like little cups inside of my skin. Again I reached into my bag and pulled out some remaining pieces of towels from when I had treated Lance's gunshot wound. I cried out as I pressed hard onto my own wounds in an attempt to stop the bleeding. My head began to ache and my thoughts became dizzy. And then I succumbed to the darkness of unconsciousness.

Eventually, I was awakened by light, a bright and beautiful light. As I stood, I saw that I was outside. And there it was. The Mountain. I'm not sure if it was Mt. Elbert or some other mountain, the name did not matter this time. Its beauty was almost more than I could take in. Around me I could see thousands upon thousands of other people, each gazing at its beauty, each filing through the large gate that welcomed us into its sanctuary. The open gate was guarded by two beings that looked more celestial than human. Their arms were opened wide, while their eyes embraced each person entering the gate. I was in a position where I could see the closeness of the gate while at the same time standing off, able to see the crowds of travelers coming toward their promise. I realized that this was not real, that I must be in the midst of a dream.

I scanned the majesty of the mountain. Its sides were shining in the sun, gleaming like walls of gold. The path through the gate beamed like a rainbow as if it were lined with soft sea glass, kind to the feet and yet sparkling in blue, green, yellow and amber. The light and the reflections were so bright, and yet they did not hurt my eyes. In fact, I could not look away.

"It's time to go," a voice to my right said. I turned and saw David. For the first time since I left him, I saw him

clearly; his dark skin and long, straight dark hair; his dark
brown eyes revealing windows of love and wisdom; his
white teeth encased in soft, pink lips.

"David," I said.

"Come," he replied. And then he held out his hand
to me. I grabbed it and let him lead me toward the gate. We
joined the others as they walked toward the entry with the
otherworldly beings. We watched those before us as they
poured through the portal. When it was our turn, one of the
guards met with my eyes.

"Stop," he said.

"Why?" I asked. My eyes wrestled with him. I so
wanted to enter.

"The gate is narrow on the road that leads to life,"
the being said.

"But others are going through," I said. I watched as
David poured through the gate with the others.

"David!" I yelled. But he could not hear me. He
kept walking, seemingly thinking that I was still next to
him.

"David!" And then he was gone. And so was The
Mountain.

My eyes gradually opened to the smell of cooking
and the soft light of a fire burning. I was lying on top of
something soft, and was covered in clean linens.
Underneath, my body was clean and clothed in the soft
white fabric of loose fitting pants and a long-sleeved shirt. I
felt for Hope. She had grown; I had been here for a long,
long time, and I was not alone.

19

Jake

I could see all four walls in the tiny room. Whoever
had rescued me was no longer here. In the glow of the
cooking fire, I could see that this shack was a home. I was
on a small cot against the far right wall, lying on my side,
facing a small woodstove anchored against the left side of
the small room. In the middle against the back wall was a
table with one chair, and against the front wall, the door that
once protected me from the ravenous dogs. The door! It was
unlocked. Whoever had been here, whoever had been caring
for me was planning on returning. I got up to lock the door.
Even though this person had worked hard to save me, how
could I be sure that after I healed, the intruder wouldn't use
me or harm me in some way? As I attempted to pull myself
up, I felt the ripping of stitches or scabs or something
coming from my right thigh. The intense pain caused me to

cry out and lay back down. I wrestled with wanting to shut out my savior and being too weak to allow him to re-enter my shelter. Giving up, I lay back, prepared to succumb.

I called out in defeat, "I have nothing left! I am nothing! I surrender!"

With my confession released, I closed my eyes and waited. Moments later, the door slowly opened. I watched as a man entered the shack. Without even looking at me, he closed the door and turned to take off his coat, which he hung on a hook to the right of the door. He walked over to the wood stove and picked up a ladle, stirring the food he was preparing in the pot. For the first time since I had awakened, my senses came alive and I appreciated its aroma, becoming distracted in my hunger. Without turning around he spoke.

"Are you ready to eat?"

"Yes," I answered. For some strange reason, I was not afraid.

"Good," he replied.

I watched as he spooned some of his recipe into a bowl and set it on the table. As he approached me, I saw the power in his eyes and in his size, and I froze in fear. His big arms reached down and lifted me to a seated position gently, without the pain I'd experienced when I tried to do it myself.

"Thank you," I said.

He did not reply, but instead just handed me the wooden bowl filled with some type of stew and a metal spoon. Starving, I took a bite. It was delicious.

"What is this?"

"Venison."

"You mean the deer are back too?" I asked excitedly.

"The ones who didn't starve," he said. I continued to eat until I had devoured the entire contents in my bowl. My stomach was quickly filled from the shock of real food. I sat the empty bowl next to me on the cot.

"Who are you?" I asked, while studying his face.

"Jake," was all he said as he got up and prepared a bowl of food for himself. I watched as he sat at the small table.

He was a big, burly man with dark curly hair and a matching dark curly beard. He wore a flannel shirt and jeans with work boots caked in mud. As I watched him lift his spoon to his mouth, I noted his large hands, powerful and skilled in their appearance. He was a man of action, not words. I imagined fuzzy images of him feeding me, caring for me. I wondered again how long I had been here. Weeks? Months?

"Why did you save me?" I asked.

"You needed help."

"How did you find me?"

"This is my shack."

"Are you the one who told me to run here? Did you see what happened, did you see my friend?"

"No."

"How long have I been here?"

"A long time," he replied.

"But how long?" I needed to know. I could feel the growth in Hope; I knew it had been a while. Was David still waiting for me in Wheeling, or had he given up? I needed to check my phone to see if there were any more messages.

"Do you have my phone?"

"Next to you on the floor."

I looked down over the edge of the bed. My backpack was sitting there unzipped and ready for my inspection. I stuck my hand inside and felt the water bottles, my gun, the map, the small food remnants, and deep at the bottom, my phone. Hurriedly, I pulled it out and pressed its power button, but there was no message, no power. I lay it beside me and looked again at Jake.

"Your baby's coming soon," he said.

"How do you know?" I asked.

"It's time," he replied.

"Time for what?"

"Time to change everything."

Where had I heard those words before? Why did they sound familiar? I was so tired of things I didn't understand, things that came to me in bits and pieces. I needed answers and I needed them now.

"I don't understand what you mean," I said. "What is going to change? Is the sun going to come back like the animals did? Is everything going to come back? Are we all going to be okay?"

"No," he said.

"Well, what does that mean?"

"Return to your people."

"What people? I don't have anyone," I said with remorse. "I am alone."

"You are never alone," he said.

I've heard that before too, I thought. But before I could say anything else to Jake, he got up, collected our dishes and placed them on the table, turned to put on his coat and opened the door. Before he walked out, he turned to me one last time.

"It's time," he said. And then he left.

I lay there alone, wrestling with his words and their conviction. *What does he mean it's time? What does he mean that everything will change? How does he know my baby is coming soon?* I carefully sat on the edge of the bed. Slowly, I rose to a standing position. I had a bad limp, but I could walk. I moved over to the hook by the door. Hanging there were my coat, hat and gloves. On the floor were my boots. Everything had been washed clean. I carried them back to the bed and slowly began to dress. I walked to the stove and saw a small basin filled with water. I rinsed my face and hands before piling my long hair into my woolen hat. I returned to the bed to sit down and organize my things. I refilled my backpack with the items I had previously removed, stuffing my gun into my coat pocket and my iPhone into the front pocket of my pants. Limping over to the stove, I filled my almost empty box of Lucky Charms with half of the remaining stew. I left the rest for Jake, if he planned on returning that is. And then I opened the door to the shack and took a deep breath, leaving the warmth of the small shelter for the coldness of the outside. The air still held its ashen mist, and it remained dark, only showing me the shadows of trees and debris. Yet I knew which way to turn, and I knew where I was going. I was still heading to Wheeling. I still believed he would be there. I believed that David was waiting for me and Hope, and that I had to get there before she was born. I wasn't sure how I would make it with a prominent limp, no companions, and ever-present danger, but I knew I had to try.

I turned left to head back toward route 70, when I was stopped dead in my tracks. There, standing against a large tree, was Hadassah's hunting rifle, the one I had given her, and Lance's motorcycle, fully assembled and ready to go.

20

Water

I walked over to the tree and touched the items, verifying their physical reality. *Not a vision*, I thought. *Real*. "Lance!" I called out. "Lance, are you here? Where are you?" But there was no answer. I picked up Hadassah's rifle. It was clean and reloaded. I slipped it through an outer loop on my backpack and secured it. Next I placed my hands on the sides of the motorcycle and pulled it from the tree. I had only ridden a motorbike once before, on my thirteenth birthday. My parents had taken Ben and me on a weekend vacation to the Pocono Mountains. The small cabin we rented had two trail bikes, which, in my eyes, made the entire trip a huge success. Shortly after our arrival, I talked my dad into taking our first ride. He hopped on a yellow Yamaha 80 while I straddled a red Honda SL-70.

Hollow Land

My dad showed me how to hold the clutch and kick start the engine. After the engine started, he taught me how to let out the clutch slowly while easing into first gear. I was a natural; and if I could do it then, I could do it now.

I went to lift my right leg in an attempt to sit on the seat, but was immediately stopped by excruciating pain in my thigh. I placed my hands on the handlebars and rolled the bike's wheels, moving it and turning it around, then once again leaning it against the tree. Now, carefully lifting my left leg, and using the tree as an anchor, I sat down on the seat. *Great,* I thought, recognizing that the kick start was on my right; I would have to endure the pain. I pulled in the clutch with my left hand and made sure I was in neutral. Next I slowly lifted my right leg and took a deep breath. I held it in to help me battle the pain, I pressed down on the starter. Nothing. I would need to kick harder. Again I took a deep breath and kicked as hard as my wounded leg would allow. I felt pain as parts of my healing wound pulled apart. My cry was stifled with the sound of an engine. It worked. Lance's engine worked. I didn't know how he fixed it or how it got here, but at that moment I didn't care about the details. I had a working motorcycle and a destination. I was on my way to Wheeling to find David, and I was only a few miles away. The headlight illuminated my trail as I cut through trees and brush on my way back to route 70. I slowed until I found a pathway to the highway, and then I found myself on the open road. I felt free. I felt hopeful. I felt alive.

At first I was timid in my driving, but soon gained confidence and pulled harder on the throttle, still travelling slowly enough to dodge debris left on the road. As I drove, I saw sporadic shadows along the sides of the road; I was not alone. Occasionally, I would see an abandoned car, but from the opened doors and my past experiences, I knew that they

135

would be emptied and without value. As I pulled the throttle, again words came to me, "run with perseverance the race marked out for you." I had heard those words before too, when I was being chased by the evil that raped me. But now, I did not feel the weight within that before stifled my escape. Now I was free, and I was in the lead. A sign was coming ahead...*Wheeling visitor center next right*. I had made it. This race I had won.

I turned right off of the highway and downshifted to slow both my impulsiveness and my speed. I took Route 2 until it became Main Street. It was at this point when I realized that I did not know which way to turn. I continued until I reached the top of a small bridge. I could hear the sound of moving water underneath. I stopped and shifted into neutral. I needed some time to think. *Where would David go? Where would he plan to meet me?* And then it hit me, the hospital. Knowing that I would soon be ready to deliver Hope, David would meet me at the hospital. Not that anyone was there, but perhaps some medical supplies would still be on hand. Hadassah had shown me the location of Wheeling Hospital on the map; I knew which way to go. Once again, ignited with direction I pulled in the clutch and prepared to shift into action. But just as I was about to let out the throttle, someone approached me from behind and threw me from the bike.

I fell hard to the ground and onto my injured right side. As I writhed in pain, another person lifted me and tossed me over the small bridge. I felt all hope fade away as my body slipped into the cool water below, and as I slowly began my descent into the water's dark depths, I felt Hope kick me with her life. It sparked my fight. It exploded my arms and legs into action. I fought for her. I fought for me. I was not yet ready to die. Currents lifted me and carried me, allowing me to occasionally take small breaths. I felt my body roll along, turning over and over, being swiftly carried downstream. I gasped for air when the waters allowed, and rested as the currents pressed on. I had to stay awake. I had to focus on breathing, just breathing. It seemed like minutes, and then hours, as my energy began to fade. I tried to fight, I really did; but the battle went on too long. I was so tired. My breaths became fewer, my struggle weaker.

"Over here!" I heard someone call out.

"Swim to this side!" the voice said.

I churned my arms and legs as I fought to make it to the voice.

"You can do it; you're almost here!" it said.

Hope kicked and I fought. The voice grew closer. It became a person. The person grabbed my arms and pulled me out of the water. Pulled me to safety.

I lay on the banks of the river and gasped for air. I touched Hope's sanctuary and found her safe. I turned on my side and coughed out air and water.

"Sarah," the voice said.

My eyes slowly lifted to meet those of my rescuer.

"David," I said. And then I closed them in the veil of exhaustion.

21

Repentance

I could feel him gently lift me off of the ground, and then I felt my body move up and down with his footsteps. Where were we going? Why did he feel the need to carry me away? Couldn't we just stop? Couldn't we just be? I tried to say his name, to open my eyes, but I was too weak and it didn't matter. I had found him; or rather he had found me. Perhaps we had found each other. I allowed myself to melt into his arms.

I awakened to the warmth of a small fire; its smoldering flames ample enough to provide heat, yet small enough to detract much notice. I was lying inside the warm protection of a sleeping bag. I tried to remember where I was, what had happened. I remembered Jake, Hadassah, the motorcycle, the water…David; did it all happen or was it a dream?

"Sarah," it was his voice. I turned to look at him. He was lying coverless on the floor next to me. He sat up when he saw that I was awake.

"Are you okay? Do you need anything?" he asked.

I looked up at him. His long, dark hair fell around his face and his dark brown eyes were alert and clear in purpose. He looked strong and convicted.

"Where are we?" I asked. I still wasn't sure if it was all real.

"On the roof of a building, across from the hospital," he said. "I can lock it off from others. It is safe here."

I was trying to collect my senses, recall all that had happened. "How did you find me?" I asked him. "How's Jack? Is he okay?" I spoke loudly and quickly thinking of the boy I had regrettably left behind. "Claire!" I continued in my panic. "Is everyone safe from Claire?"

"Jack's fine; strong as ever; they all are. Claire is long gone. Everyone is safe. We can talk about them later," he said. "Right now, let's just think about you. How can I help? What can I do?"

Slowly, I propped myself up onto my elbows and then to a seated position. "I'm okay," I said. "I'm really okay." And I was. I wanted nothing more than to jump into his arms, to hold him, to tell him that I loved him, but something prompted me to wait.

"I can't believe I found you," he said interrupting my thoughts. "I mean in a way I knew that I would; I had to, but still, now that you're here, that we're together…" I saw his eyes begin to fill. Small trickles of emotion spilled down his cheeks. "I love you Sarah, and I am so thankful that I am finally man enough to tell you. When you're ready, I have so much more that I have to say; so much to confess." He handed me some water and I drank eagerly. Then I set the empty bottle aside and looked up into his eyes.

"I'm ready now." I no longer wanted any uncertainties in our words. It was time to get everything out in the open.

He gently brushed the side of my face with the fingertips of his strong hands. "I'm so grateful that I found you, that I got a second chance. But at the same time, Sarah, I feel so dirty, so full of shame."

"We both have things to confess," I said.

"No," he said. "I failed you. That last night," he briefly looked away, "I was trying so hard to find you, to talk to you." He placed his hands on his face and rubbed his eyes. He pushed his hair back and I could see the weariness and the weight he had been carrying.

"You did find me," I said.

"Yes," he replied with look of relief, "I found you. Thanks be to God, I found you."

He leaned close to me and looked into my eyes, letting me know that his words were truth and meant only for me.

"Sarah, I was a fool and a coward in keeping away from you. I loved you from the time we both first met. Actually, I loved you when I first dreamt of you, before we even physically met. In the dream, a voice told me to wait for you, that you were the one, and that you were coming. But I was afraid; I was afraid for so many reasons. In my past I had seen what love could do; how it could hurt. I thought distance could protect us both, so I hid in my relationship with Claire; I hid from love in staying away from you. In my weakness, I failed our dream, but more importantly, I failed you." He briefly closed his eyes to gather his plea. Upon reopening them, he spoke the words that in some ways I always knew.

"Sarah, I am in love with you. I always have been, and I always will be. Please forgive me for being a coward. Please forgive me if I hurt you. I will understand if you choose not to return my love; I just needed to confess mine to you, for you to know why I had foolishly turned away, to make sure that you were safe."

"I know that you love me," I said. "I always knew. I just couldn't accept only a part of your love; for it to be right, I mean. The type of love that was real, that means something more than just sex or companionship." For the first time I felt wholly confident and worthy of not just his love, but of everyone's.

"You're right," he said. "And I knew that too. Claire's hold on me was not her fault, or anyone else's; it was mine. It was my sin. My self-worth revolved around protecting all of the women in my life; first my mother, then my sister Jenna, and then Claire, and even you. You were strong Sarah, you didn't need me in the way the others did; and it scared me. I thought that the best way I could protect you was to stay away. And then because I had failed to save first my mother, and then later Jenna; Claire, in her weakness, became my unhealthy obsession. I confused protection with relationship, and my relationship with her was wrong. And that stain was there long before I met you; it began when Claire and I were just kids who confused sex with security. I hope that you can in some way understand my flaws, and maybe even some day forgive me for them. I was weak, and immature, and Sarah," he said as he looked at me, "I'm sorry. I am so sorry. Even if you can never forgive me, I just needed you to know."

I watched as the tension in his face eased, and he closed his eyes, finally free of his burden.

"I do forgive you," I said.

And I knew then that I, too, needed to ask for forgiveness.

"I'm not innocent either," I said. "Just like you, in my insecurities, I turned to Lance. I was with him even though I didn't love him. I was with him when I only ever loved you. It was unfair to all three of us. I tried to hurt you, to make you jealous, and in the process I hurt us all."

"Is Lance okay; is he still alive?" David asked quietly.

"Yes," I answered. "He's with a new group. They're headed south."

"Good," he said.

"David," I continued, "There's more that I need to tell you, much more."

Keeping his eyes closed he nodded his head. "Sarah," he said, "you don't owe me any explanations. The past is over, and none of it matters anymore."

I'm sure he was preparing for me to tell him the story of my past relationship, the one that had caused my pregnancy. Would he feel relieved or disgusted to know that it wasn't a relationship at all, but that I had been raped by four strangers, that I didn't even know the father of my child?

"No," I said, "There are some things that I need for you to know. If we are going to have a life together, we can't hold any more secrets." And so I told him.

"The day after the explosion," I began, "I was raped."

I watched as his eyes opened wide and looked wild with pain and anger.

"What?" he cried out. "Sarah, my God, why didn't you tell me?"

"Please, just listen," I said. I wanted to get it all out. It was time for each of us to lay our burdens down.

"I was raped by four strangers. They killed my friend first, and then they attacked me. I was left for dead, until Jack and his father found me. They nursed me back to life. It was weeks after this that Jack and I met you and the others. I didn't know that the attack had left me pregnant; how could I have known? I was eighteen-years-old, worlds away, so I thought, of even thinking of what it might be like to be pregnant. That last night, the one when you came looking for me, that was when I realized...that I knew. Ruth told me. She made me see. I was in shock. I couldn't believe it. I didn't know what to do. And then you heard me; David you heard me say it when I wasn't even ready to hear it myself. Worse, you repeated it. I heard the apprehension in your voice. I imagined what you must have thought of me. I was so ashamed; I couldn't face you."

"But Sarah, it wasn't your fault," he said. "And no matter what had caused your pregnancy, none of it was going to change what I had to say to you. I loved you no matter what. Even then, even before I knew."

I realized that David never saw me as soiled; I was the only one who had labeled myself.

"I need you to understand why I left," I said. "Even though I knew that it wasn't my fault and that I shouldn't have felt ashamed, I was so lost and confused. I felt like I could never face you, Jack, Ruth or the others again. And in that moment of crisis, Lance came to me. He told me that he was okay with my being pregnant, that he was happy that I was bringing in a new life, that it was one good thing in all of the bad. I didn't feel so awful about it then. He promised he'd take me away and take care of me. I was in such shock and so disgusted and afraid, that his offer sounded good; it seemed like a solution, so I accepted. And then he made advances, and I, too, confused sex for security. Then you saw us; you saw me. You saw me with him. I could only imagine what you thought of me then. I loved you so much, and I knew that you had once loved me, but at that moment I couldn't imagine our love surviving either of our infidelities. I couldn't accept your love within the realm of Claire, and likewise I was sure that you couldn't accept mine in the realm of Lance. So I left. I thought walking away was the best thing I could do for us both. I was a coward too, and it has always been a bad habit of mine…walking away, that is, avoiding painful encounters." I thought of my father's death, my coldness in it all. It felt so good to confess the ills of my past. I finally felt free from it all.

"If we had only told each other the truth," he said, "from the very beginning."

"I don't think we fully understood the truth at the time," I said.

"But we do now," he said. "Now we can have a whole new beginning."

I looked up at the lifeless sky. It seemed strange to talk about new beginnings in the midst of the end. Yet, I felt it too, and I wanted it to be free from darkness.

"David, that night, before I left, I came to see you one last time. You were asleep by the fire. Where was Claire?" I needed to be certain that she was out of his life.

"I don't know," he said. "Earlier that day, I had ended our relationship. I told Claire that while I would always protect her, that I didn't love her; not in the way that was right. I told her that I only loved you in that way, and that I wanted only you. She threatened to kill herself like she did thousands of times before when I tried to break free of her, but this time I didn't allow myself to be consumed by her deception. This time I walked away. I went looking for you, to ask for your forgiveness. That was when I found you, first with Ruth, and then later with Lance."

"David, I'm so sorry. You must have felt so confused."

"Sure I did," he said. "But it didn't change my mind. I love you. I was ready to fight for you."

"And then I hid," I said softly and with some pangs of shame.

"You did," he laughed. "But I found you anyway, didn't I?"

"Yes," I smiled, "you did."

"Will you marry me Sarah?"

What? Had I heard him correctly?

"I want to spend whatever time I have left with you, completely and wholly with you. Sarah," he asked again, "will you marry me?"

"Yes."

I watched his face light into a full smile, his happiness fully exposed. I smiled back at him as I rolled onto my side. With my quite large and growing mid-section lying along the rooftop, and hair and body mixed with ash and dirty river water; I was sure that I didn't look so appealing, certainly not like the typical woman on the cover of a bridal magazine. But he didn't seem to notice.

"I love you Sarah," he said. "I love you with all that I am."

His words made me realize the irony of all my fruitless searches for love. Love had actually found me.

"When?" he asked.

He broke me away from my thoughts. "When what?" I responded.

"When will you marry me?"

"Well," I joked, "I'm not really all that busy right now."

He smiled and said, "Perfect. I've already written my vows."

J.E.Byrne

"Impressive," I said.

"Well, I've had quite a bit of alone time while searching the dark lands of West Virginia for you," he added.

I laughed, struggling to rise toward him. He gently laid his hand on my shoulder, encouraging me to stay at rest. Instead, he turned onto his side, and lowered his head to the ground, meeting me right where I was. And then he began.

"Through this season of
darkness, I desired you,
but at first, I would not let
myself find you.

And then I walked this
hollow land, searching for
you,
but my sin would not let
me find you.

While on my journey, a
stranger intervened,
to whom I confessed my
faithlessness,
and was directed in my
path.

And so now together on
this day of our wedding,
I vow to cherish and honor
you,
my love and my wife,

And if you will allow, to
the child you are carrying,
I vow to cherish and honor,
as my child, of my own
flesh."

My heart was stirred. I felt the flush of passion
redden my cheeks and fill my chest. I was speechless.
    "Too much?" he asked.
    "You wrote that?"
    "Yeah," he confessed. "Since the time that I left the
group to search for you, I've been keeping a journal. I
wanted to record all of my thoughts and the words I hoped
to share with you, in case something happened…in case we
never did meet again. Then one night, when I was sitting up
here, on watch for your arrival, words just kind of forced
their way into my mind.
It almost felt like a dream or a vision. They became
imprinted upon my heart and so I quickly wrote them down,
experimenting with them, placing them into the verse that I
read to you. Sounds crazy doesn't it?"
    "No," I said with a knowing smile, "it doesn't
sound crazy at all."
    But something was more pressing then his muse.
"David, you said that you want to be my child's father. Did
that come from the dream or vision too, or was that from
just you?"
    "All me. Sarah, the child is a part of you, so it
already is a part of me."
    "David," I began, "I don't have any eloquent vows
prepared, all I can say is that I have loved you since the
beginning, since the first time we were alone. Do you
remember when we were in the abandoned school, when we

realized that we had each dreamed of one another, even before we had formally met?" He nodded and smiled.

"I knew then," I continued, "that I was in love with you, but it wasn't until now that I realized the depth of that love. I want nothing more than to live our remaining days as your wife, and with you as Hope's father."

"Hope?" he asked.

"That's what I've named her. Do you like it?"

"Are you kidding?" he said. "I love it! Today, I have been blessed with Hope; a beautiful daughter named Hope."

"How do you know she'll be beautiful?" I joked.

"Because you're her mother," he said. "May I now pronounce us husband and wife, so that I can finally kiss you?" he asked.

"You may," I said. He leaned over and kissed me softly on the lips. The kiss lingered. I wove my fingers around the nape of his neck and I pulled him closer, teasing my fingertips in the softness of his hair. The kiss of true love is unique. Yes, it's passionate, but it is so much more. It is complete. In its moment it is like nothing else exists; only you and him, with both lives finally placed within the same story. The story of us.

And then I jumped a bit because Hope kicked me hard in the side. I placed my hand on top of her. "David, would you like to touch, to feel your daughter?"

"I would," he said. I gently lifted his hand and placed it on top of Hope. Beneath his touch she kicked and proved herself his child. I watched as his face softened in the gift of her life. He looked at me as we celebrated our first moment as husband and wife, mother and father.

"I love you," he said. "Both of you."

"We love you too," I said back.

And then the pains began.

22

Birth

"David," I cried out as sharp pain spread over my abdomen.

He grasped my hand. "What is it? What's wrong?"

"I think she's coming now," I said. "But it's too soon, it hasn't been long enough."

I hoped that the pains would stop, that maybe I could will them off so that Hope would have more time to grow. But they continued to advance. David let go of my hand and got up to move.

"Don't leave me!" I cried. "I'm scared."

"I will never leave you again," he said. "I'm just going to grab some things that I collected from the hospital."

"How did you know?" I asked as the sharp pains subsided, giving me a few moments of reprieve.

"A stranger that I met told me what to do, how to prepare, that our child would be coming soon."

"You mean the stranger in your vows wasn't a metaphor?"

"No, I'm not the intellectual you are," he said. "The person was real."

I wanted to ask him more about the stranger, where he had met him and how he had known, but the pains returned and wouldn't allow me any more conversation. David returned several times with clean towels, bandages, water and other supplies. When he had exhausted his assemblage, he sat by my side.

"What can I do?" he asked. "How can I help?"

I had begun breathing rapidly and sweat was beading along my forehead and upper lip. Before I could answer, another sharp pain hit. I cried out. I had seen plenty of movies and TV shows with women giving birth, but none of them was anything close to accurate. The pain was unbearable, and all I hoped for was that it would stop. David whispered words of comfort, but there was nothing he could do to lessen my pain. I was alone in this struggle, or so I thought. As the next contraction hit, words flashed before my eyes and strangely, I spoke them aloud: "Before I formed you, I knew you. Before you were born, I set you apart..."

Pain cut me off in mid-sentence, but somehow David was able to complete the vision. "I appointed you to be a prophet to the nations," he said aloud as he gently placed his hand on top of Hope. The pain once again subsided.

"You saw?" I asked.

"Yes," he said. "And they demanded to be spoken."

I nodded my head. I understood what had happened to him; after all, this type of occurrence had colored my path since the explosion. As I awaited the next wave of contractions, for the first time I took comfort in the strange words by the persistent Author. Being deeply known by someone gave me a feeling of purpose and substance. It calmed me. When the next pain hit, I was able to breathe deeply into it. I realized that the better I could endure the pain, the safer it would be for my health and for Hope's birth. I could feel David at my side. He had a cool cloth and was gently wiping my forehead.

"I love you," he repeated. "You're doing a great job. It has to almost be over."

But it wasn't. Pain after pain came upon me. It was exhausting and I didn't know how much longer I could endure. I couldn't hold down the sips of water David tried to give me even though I was dehydrated beyond safety. I was growing weaker and weaker as the pains increased. It seemed as though there were only seconds between them.

"David," I said. "I think it's time. I could feel a new pressure in my lower abdomen.

"Okay," he answered. "What should I do? How can I help?"

I raised my knees and prepared my body and position for birth.

"Please," I whispered between breaths, "just be sure to catch her when she comes out." I tried to give him a smile, but it was difficult to mask the pain. I watched as he moved himself between my legs and prepared to meet his daughter. He looked into my eyes and smiled. "I love you Sarah. I love you both."

I was in such a state of pain and exhaustion that I couldn't even gather any modesty for my new husband. Instead I began to push, groaning in the discomfort, yet knowing that I trusted him completely, and it was he, David, who would help me get through it. Again I felt that it was time for me to push, to push my Hope into a post-apocalyptic world; to bring birth into death; but I was so tired, the pain had gone on for too long.

"I can't do it," I cried out to him. "I've got nothing left."

"You can do it, Sarah. You are stronger than you think." Where had I heard those words before? Why did everything keep repeating itself? *I will try,* I thought to myself. *By God I will try.* With the next pain I took a deep breath and I pushed. My voice cried out in the rawness of struggle.

"I see her," he said. "She's coming."

I looked up at him with weary eyes. "Can you," I said between breaths, "can you pull her? Can you help me?" I could see worry in his eyes but I wasn't strong enough to ask any more questions. I watched as he placed his hands on top of my stomach and raised his head to the blackened sky.

"Please don't take her away from me, not when we've just found one another. Help her. Help her in the ways that I can't. Save her, please save them both."

And then the urge to push consumed me and I focused all of my remaining energy into this one last act. And then I heard the cries of an infant. And then everything went black.

23

Hope

I awakened to a tiny being, clean and wrapped in warm linens, suckling at my breast. David was at my side. He looked beautiful...a little worried, yes, but gorgeous still.

"Sarah," he said with a relieved smile.

"Have you just been sitting there staring at me until I woke up?" I asked in a groggy voice.

"Yes," he admitted. "And thank you for not taking too long." He leaned over and kissed my lips while laying a gentle hand on his daughter's tiny back. "You did great Sarah. Look at her; she's perfect."

I looked down at my beautiful daughter who was illuminated by the light of our rooftop fire. She was very small, but pink and according to her ravenous appetite, just as feisty as her mother.

"I can't believe she's here," I said. *Something so beautiful coming from something so awful,* I thought. I brushed my lips along her soft head, feeling the fuzzy newness of her hair. Her tiny mouth was tugging at my breast. It felt so natural. I mean, here I was, an unprepared eighteen-year-old mother, and yet my body seemed to know how to perform. It was like all I had to do was show up, and the miracle of biology took care of the details. It was as it should be. I took my hand and protectively nestled it around her tiny body.

"She's a miracle," David said as if he had been reading my thoughts. He handed me a glass filled with some type of thick-looking concoction inside. "Drink," he said.

"What is it?" I asked.

"Some type of vitamin drink," he answered. "To keep both of you healthy and strong."

"Wow, where did you find this?" I asked, impressed that such a valuable source of nutrition was in my very own hand.

"In the hospital," he said. "Wheeling hospital is across the street."

Wheeling Hospital. I thought of Hadassah, the location where she was both lost and saved. *How significant,* I thought, *that through her guidance and sacrifice, it would become a source of life for me.*

"How did you know to go there? Where to find this? Where to find me?" I asked.

"I met a woman," he said.

"Excuse me," I responded. "Please explain."

"The stranger from my vows," he said, "was a she."

"And *she* was travelling alone?" I asked.

"Yes," he continued. "And I think that she was looking for me."

I turned my eyes away from Hope and toward him. "You said she was a stranger. How could that be?" I asked.

"I don't know," he admitted. "After separating from the group to find you, I got lost. I was aimlessly travelling along route 70, remembering that Lance seemed determined to set your course southeast."

"Sorry about sending you on a wild goose chase," I said.

"Sarah, it was no wild chase. I was determined to find you."

I smiled at him. "Is that when you met her?" I asked.

"One morning," he continued, "while I was searching in the wooded area off of the highway, I found what I thought was Lance's sleeping bag, and it was covered in blood. Panicked, I grabbed it and headed for the road. It was then that I heard the sound of footsteps. I listened attentively, noting that they revealed only one person. I had to call out; after all, I thought, it could have been you, and from what I found I knew that you needed help. So with a weapon in one hand for protection, I yelled out to the stranger. A female voice answered. She said that she was alone, and was of no danger to me. Sarah, I thought the voice was yours. I was so elated that I dropped the sleeping bag and found myself running out onto the road shouting your name. The person lit a candle and I could see in the light that although she was a woman not much older than you, she was someone I did not know. Yet, she smiled as if she knew me, as if she had been searching for me. 'David,' she said."

"Who was it?" I asked excitedly as I interrupted him. "What was her name?" I tried to think who it could have been. Eva was the only one who came to mind.

"She didn't say," he answered.

"Did she have short punky hair?" I asked. "Was she Asian?"

I watched as he tried to remember the woman's face. "No," he said.

I felt really confused. Who had I met that I had so soon forgotten?

David continued, "I asked her how she knew me. Instead of answering right away, she asked me to sit and join her for some food and water while she explained. I told her that I couldn't, that I was looking for someone who needed my help. As I turned to go, she revealed that she knew who I was looking for. She said your name, Sarah; she *knew* you. I quickly turned around, and walked toward her, taking a seat next to where she had positioned herself on the ground. I asked her where you were, and told her of finding the sleeping bag covered with blood. She assured me that she had recently been with you, and that you were safe, but that you would soon be giving birth. I asked her if you were travelling with a man named Lance. She said no, that you were with someone named Jake who was helping you to get to Wheeling. She told me that I should go to the Wheeling Hospital and load up on the supplies I would need for your birth and survival. She outlined for me exactly what to get and where I would find it. She even instructed me on how to deliver the baby, what to do and how to care for you both. I asked her why she had left you, that with all of her medical knowledge why didn't *she* stay with you. She said that *I* was the one to deliver the child, that *I* was the one to keep you safe. She said that you had sent her on a mission to find me and direct me to Wheeling and to wait for you there. I hurried to leave. I thought that maybe I could find you and Jake along the way, before we all got to Wheeling, but the woman was firm in telling me that I instead needed to carry out all of the instructions she gave, that your life depended on it. I was to spend the next few days taking all the medical supplies to the rooftop across from the hospital. This way I could see over the main streets and watch for your arrival. She told me that you would be arriving on a motorcycle and that you would be there in three days."

"She said that *I* sent her? David, try to remember; what did she look like?" I asked.

"I'm not sure," David said. "I mean, she was not much older than you. She was pale and thin, and I think she had long black hair. I do remember that she had sad eyes; large, sad eyes."

Hadassah? I thought. *But it couldn't be.*

I looked up at David as he continued with his account. "As strange as it all sounded, I believed her. I mean, how could she have made it all up? She knew my name, she knew so much about you and your condition. So with purpose and hope, I thanked her and got up to head to Wheeling. With my back turned from her for just an instant, I asked her if she would come with me. But when I turned back to get her answer, she was gone. Just like that Sarah, she had disappeared. So I quickly made off with my journey, did everything she said, and then waited here for you. And Sarah, everything then happened exactly as she said it would."

Hadassah, I thought. *How could this be?* I wondered. *I saw her die. I watched as the wild dogs took her down. There was no way she could have survived. It doesn't make any sense. Just like it doesn't make sense that she knew that Jake had found me and nursed me back to health. Just like it doesn't make sense that a working motorcycle...Lance's working motorcycle mind you, met me as I limped out of the shack, surely unable to successfully walk to Wheeling. Just like it doesn't make sense that*

157

Hadassah told David to go to Wheeling, specifically where to wait for me, and even how to prepare for Hope's delivery. This was all too much. I could not wrap my head around what seemed to be supernatural influence.

"David," I said, "I did set out to find you with someone named Hadassah. She looked like your description of the woman, but she was killed by a pack of wild dogs. I know it; I saw it. I watched her die. There was no one else. I told no one to find you and send you to Wheeling."

David turned his face away from me as he tried to take in my words.

"When did you send me the text to meet you in Wheeling?" I asked. I thought maybe if I got some perspective of timing, it could help me understand these seemingly abstract events. Hadassah had been with me when I received his message.

"Sarah," he said. "I never sent you a text."

"Yes you did," I insisted. "The text that told me to meet you in Wheeling."

"My phone hasn't turned on since the explosion," he said.

What was going on? I did see a text telling me to go to Wheeling, didn't I?

My thoughts travelled back to my time in Jake's shack. I wondered how long I had been there; if David had been near when he met the woman, if she could have been Hadassah. I thought back to meeting Jonathan and Elizabeth all those months ago, how they, like Jake and Hadassah, had provided for us and then mysteriously vanished.

David gently touched my face. "Maybe she was friends with Jonathan and Elizabeth." I looked up at him.

"Maybe she was," I said. Hope squiggled at my side reminding me of the life each of these others in some way had preserved. I decided to focus on the gift, and not lose myself in the process. I felt incredibly grateful.

"David, could you help me to lift Hope, so that I can see her?"

His large hands gently lifted our child. I looked closely into her tiny face.

"She has the shape of your eyes," he said.

"Yes," I agreed.

"And your strength," he added.

"Oh, she has much more than that," I said. I realized that she held the promise of life and the blessing of someone or something that I did not yet fully understand. I smiled at her and I could swear she smiled back. I lifted my arms and accepted her tiny weight from David's. I lay her again on my chest where she fed until she dropped off into sleep. My eyes became heavy as the weight of childbirth began to set in.

"You should sleep too," David said after forcing me to down some more of the raunchy tasting, but highly nutritious hospital drink.

"But there's so much I want to tell you, and so much I want to hear about you, Jack, and the others," I said, even with my eyes closed. In the distraction of giving birth, I had forgotten about Leah and Claire, and the need to warn the others.

"Claire," I said becoming weak with the effort, "We need to warn the others about her."

My heightened emotions made me dizzy and began to upset Hope. I tried hard to open my eyes, but they would not acquiesce.

"Shhh," David said, encouraging me to calm. "It's okay. Claire is no longer with the group; she left. Everyone's safe…everyone's okay. How about I tell you all about us while you close your eyes and rest?" he suggested as a way to calm me. "Later, when you're stronger, it can be your turn to tell me everything, especially how you got that nasty wound on your leg. Deal?"

"Deal," I relented. I was too tired to speak or do much of anything, except to be happy, and I mean really, really happy. Even in the widening gyre of things falling apart, I felt full of hope and joy. I'll never understand the paradox of life.

"Where should I begin?" he said aloud to himself.

"The night I left," I whispered. He smiled and kissed me on the forehead.

"Okay," he repeated, "the night you left..."

24

Second Coming

"The night you left, I was searching for you, desperately hoping to ask for your forgiveness and declare my love. But as you recall," he smiled, "I was ordered to go away. But since we already spoke of that part of the story," he joked, "with your permission, I'll begin shortly after that unfortunate turn of events."

"Agreed," I said, returning his smile.

"Well, determined I would speak to you when you returned, I decided to give you some space and wait back at ground zero with the others. I sat down with Jack, Jared, Britney, and Sam by the small cooking fire. I could see Ruth and the Eirmanns off to the side, chatting as if they were old friends. I listened while the kids spoke of things as if life were normal: video games, television, movies. It was amazing. Here we were in the midst of this crazy story, and yet the four of them were behaving just like regular kids. I found it disturbing and bizarre, while at the same time, incredibly comforting. Eventually, each of them fell asleep. I decided to go out again, to look for you one more time. I went to where I had last seen you with Lance, and then earlier with Ruth. I looked throughout the perimeter of the camp, but you were nowhere to be found. It was so quiet, silent really; I knew you had fallen asleep. I figured I would let you rest and then look for you again the morning, so I headed back to the camp and lay down near the kids. I lay there for a long time, conflicted and somewhat ruined. I knew my burdens would not leave until I at least asked for your forgiveness. I'm not sure when I finally fell asleep, but I must have, because the next thing I remember was Jack pulling at my arm. He told me that you had gone, that you had left with Lance. Well, I guess you could say that I panicked. Not only had my love left me, but with him! I hated him for stealing you, of course, but more importantly; I didn't trust him. I was worried for your safety. I ran around like a crazy person, calling your name and stomping through the woods. Finally, Jack was able to calm me. He told me the gesture you made for him, a kind of inside best friends gesture, with the chocolate left by his side. He told me that it meant that you were okay, that you left by free will. It was then that we also realized that Leah was missing. Knowing that she left with you was another comfort. While both of these things slightly, and I do mean only slightly, calmed my fears for you, it of course increased my pain. I realized that you had chosen Lance over me. I realized that I had lost you. And I knew that I deserved it. But, as you obviously now know, I couldn't accept such a fate. I loved you, after all. I knew that I couldn't live without you, or at least that I didn't want to. I had to go after you. I had to fight for you."

I tried to open my eyes to interrupt David. I needed to tell him that Leah did not go with us, that she had been murdered while following us. But he was talking so fast, and I was too weak to intervene, so I just continued to listen as he told his story, waiting for the time when I could tell mine.

"Desperate, I met with the group. I told them that I was going after you. None of them tried to stop me; in fact they all encouraged me. Jack even told me not to dare come back without you. He loves you, you know."

I nodded. I felt so ashamed that in my selfish woes, I had left Jack.

"He assured me that I would find you. You know Jack," David said. "He told me he had already seen it; all of us together again I mean. It gave me great hope; Jack's visions always gave me hope. I believe in him. So everyone helped me to gather some things, and then they set me off to find you; they *all* sent me to find you. Before I left, I told them not to wait for me, but to continue on with the journey to Mt. Elbert. I was willing to die for you, but they didn't need to die for me. They decided they would stay at camp for two days, and if I didn't return, then they would continue on 70 west. We planned our next destination as one we could all easily find…the Indianapolis Speedway. So when you and Hope are strong enough, Sarah, and with your blessing, that's where we will go. We will plan to meet the others in Indianapolis."

I smiled and nodded my head, gently whispering, "Indianapolis." And then I closed my eyes and succumbed to the fatigue of childbirth. David lay down beside me, under the covers and rested his long left arm around the base of my neck and around my left shoulder. Then I felt his right arm lay gently across my midsection and rest itself gently on Hope. I felt safe, secure and content. Even in this dying land, we were a family; husband, wife, and child. We were perched on the rooftop of an abandoned building, in a world with no sun, moon, or stars, and yet we had hope; I felt hope. We were going to find the others, and we were going to continue with our journey to Mt. Elbert. And at that moment, I really believed that we were going to make it. I allowed myself to fall asleep in my optimism.

And then I had another one of my prophetic dreams. Again I saw The Mountain; again I saw it in its splendor of colors. This time I welcomed it; I embraced the dream. I wanted to be there; I wanted to go. I wanted to take Hope there, to enter its gates with my husband and child. As I approached the gate, everything looked familiar; after all, I had now visited here many times. Around me I could see legions of men, women, children, even animals for the first time, coming from all directions toward the base of its huge body. Again, I saw the ethereal guards, watching the four gateways: there was one open for people travelling from each direction; north, south, east, and west. I was so excited to be there; we all were. Everyone looked happy; everyone looked ready. This time when I approached the eastern gate, the guard did not dismiss me. I entered; I really entered through the gate and began walking up the path. I looked down and saw Hope in my arms. Ahead of me I could see Jack, Jared, and Britney. I turned my head back and saw Ruth, Sam and his father; but where was David? I couldn't see him. I turned around to walk back and find him. It became difficult as I swam against the waters of people entering through the gate; it was as though they didn't see me. Hope began to cry as people bumped her. I cried out "David! David!" But he didn't answer.

As I continued through the crowd, I looked ahead and saw first my mother, and then my father and Ben. "Mom!" I yelled. "Dad, Ben!" They came toward me with open arms. I showed them Hope. My father smiled and accepted Hope into his arms as he, my mom, and Ben kept proceeding toward the gate. I ran through the crowd calling David's name, but still there was no answer. Suddenly, I felt the ground beneath my feet begin to shake. The people around me took off hurrying toward the gates. I turned to follow them with my eyes. On the top of The Mountain I could see beams of light. They were so strong, that I had to shield my eyes. They were descending down upon the mountaintop as the earth beneath began to crack and split. Huge chasms began to appear, and I had to dodge in order to avoid falling into their tombs. I knew that if I wanted to make it, to be there when He came, that I would need to run through the gate now. I heard a voice, and it commanded me to go. And I believed the voice, so I did. I ran and ran and did not stop until I made it through the gate and toward what I could only imagine was a second coming. And David was not there.

"David," I gasped as I was startled awake from my dream.

"I'm here," he said as he tightened his arm around me.

"Please don't ever leave me," I said.

"I will never leave you," he promised.

Then I listened as his breaths returned to their patterns of sleep. I kept my hands on Hope's small body, and enjoyed the warmth of my family. I closed my eyes, but I fought desperately against sleep; I was too afraid that I would lose him again in my dreams.

25

Spiritus Mundi

Eventually, I must have given in to sleep, because I was awakened to banging on the steel door that separated us from the rest of the world. I sat up abruptly, causing Hope to stir. David was already awake and on guard. Even though the door was securely bolted, I could see David's shadow, illuminated by our small fire, armed with a rifle and standing to the left of the door. *When did he start carrying a weapon?* I wondered. *Why did everything have to turn so violent?* Hope began to make small noises, and in fear I nestled her close to my chest.

"I know someone's up there; I can smell your fire," I heard a man's voice say. "Let me up, I won't hurt you, I swear. I'm alone. I just want something to eat."

David didn't say a word. I tried to keep Hope quiet against my chest, but she kept stirring and began to make small crying noises.

"Shhh, I whispered to her. It's okay. Shhh." I tried to press her toward my breast, but she wouldn't acquiesce. David's eyes met mine as if we thought we could will her to silence. It didn't work; she began to cry the infant songs that follow the days after their sleepy births.

"Is there a baby up there?" the stranger said. "How many people do you have up there? Let me in."

"There is nothing here for you," David said.

"Where there are people there is food," the man replied.

"I have no food," David answered.

At this point Hope's cries became wails, and I could not calm her awakening. I stood up and began to rock her against my body, but still she would not quiet.

"I don't know what kind of crazy shit you've got going on up there," the man said, "but I'm not leaving until you open this door. You can't stay up there forever, and we'll be here waiting for you."

"I thought you said you were alone."

"Well, I guess I lied then didn't I," he yelled back.

"Yeah, big surprise," I heard David say to himself.

What are we going to do? I thought. *We live in a time constructed by liars, murderers, and cannibals. How will we survive? How can we protect Hope?* It all seemed pretty unlikely.

David came by me and laid his rifle down. He gently took Hope from my arms and silently motioned for me to go ahead and lay back down. I watched him as he began to gently rock Hope while walking around the perimeters of the rooftop. In time she began to quiet, and eventually she fell asleep in his arms. I took a deep breath as I watched him come near me and sit down by my side.

"David, what are we going to do?" I asked. "We only have a limited amount of food and supplies, and then

we will need to leave. How will we get past them? We don't
even know how many of them there are." I was beginning to
panic.

"Sarah," he said as he took his right arm off of
Hope and used his fingers to gently brush my hair away
from my face and tuck it behind my ear, "It will be okay.
I'm not going to let anything happen to you or Hope."

"But how?" I asked. "How can you protect us from
them? They are probably lined up with guns just waiting to
steal whatever food we have left or maybe even just to eat
us." I was beginning to panic. I had seen too much of the
horrific possibilities.

"Sarah," he repeated in a calm and quiet voice. "It
will be okay. Trust me. Somehow, I know that it will be
okay. But right now, we need for you to rest so that you will
be strong enough to help me exit here and protect Hope. Do
you understand how important it is for you to rest and
recover right now?"

"Yes," I said, realizing that he was right. My panic
was not doing us any favors. I had to put all of my energies
into quickly healing and regaining my strength. I had to be
ready for our exit from Wheeling and our journey to reunite
with the others in Indianapolis. "Are you sure they can't get
up here?"

"Yes, I'm sure," he said looking at me with
confidence. "That's why we're here. I secured this space
while I was waiting for you; it is completely protected. The
only way in and out is through that door, and no one is
getting through that iron fortress."

I looked at the door. A large iron bar was secured in
its edifice; only a superhero or an incredibly motivated
welder could get through. We were safe from the strangers
as long as we were on our side of the world. I would wait to
worry about our exit until that time came. Now, the wisest

thing I could do was rebuild my vigor for that hour. I watched as David kissed the top of Hope's head, and then lay her in the soft blankets that made up our rooftop bed. He then picked up his rifle and held it by his side, just in case, I supposed. I knew the truth: that nothing was sure anymore.

"David," I said, "When do you think we should leave?"

"Not for a while yet," he answered. "I have everything we need to last us at least another week. I want to be sure you are strong and healed before we move on."

I took a deep breath. I committed to myself that I'd do everything I could to physically prepare. I would be sure to sleep whenever Hope slept and to begin walking the perimeter of the rooftop several times a day. I was young and strong; I could bounce back quickly from childbirth and on toward survival. As I looked over at our sleeping infant, I acknowledged that it was my time to sleep. I closed my eyes to the rebirth of the stranger's presence.

"We're still here," he said. "Just didn't want you to think we forgot about you. Just open the door and pass us out some food. Then we'll leave you alone," he said.

I opened my eyes and looked at David. He just nodded his head to me indicating that there was no need to respond to the stranger's threats.

"What if he's telling the truth?" I asked. "What if we just give him some food? Do you think they'll go away and leave us alone?"

"No. We are not opening that door. Just try to tune him out."

But I couldn't. He would not stop. Every few minutes he would yell something else through the door. It was psychological torture. I couldn't understand why he wouldn't just shut up and go away.

"He's trying to break us down," David said.

"You've got to tune him out."

"I can't," I said. "I keep hearing his voice, taunting us. You've got to help me. Please distract me, talk to me, tell me a story or something. I know, tell my about your life. There's so much about you that I don't know, and I want to know it all. It would be the perfect distraction."

David smiled and then lay himself down next to Hope who was snuggled in between both of us. "Okay, my wife," he said. "Where would you like me to begin?"

"Tell me about your life as a child," I said. "Jenna told me about your parents splitting up and then abandoning you; begin after that."

"Okay," he said, "I'll begin where, as a child, I thought it had all ended; but as I now see, was just another beginning." And as he began to fill me with the shadows of his past, the incessant gnawing of the outsider faded into the distance. All I heard was David; all I knew was him.

"I was ten when my mother left. My father had long before abandoned us, but I was used to that. My mom, well that devastated me. I was just a kid, yet I suddenly saw myself as the sole protector and parent to Jenna. Jenna wanted to stay in our home, to just continue going to school, coming home, eating peanut butter and jelly sandwiches, as if nothing had changed. But I knew that everything had changed. I knew that apartments and food cost money, and that we didn't have any. I knew that kids needed to be protected by adults, and again that we didn't have any. So I talked Jenna into telling our teacher Mrs. Jackson. I thought our teacher would help, maybe even keep us as her own. I trusted her. And of course now I understand, but then, her calling the authorities and setting us up in foster care, seemed like a betrayal. I held Jenna and watched her cry while we were taken into custody and placed in a shelter with other unwanted kids. I thought my actions would protect her, but instead they only made her feel more vulnerable. For days we didn't do much other than huddle together, avoiding the other kids who seemed so rough, already significantly hardened by life."

The banging on the door began again, but I barely noticed as my heart was breaking for both Jenna and David. I was amazed that they each turned out to be so exceptional; such a light in a dark world; and their world was pretty dark even before the apocalypse. I realized that we all suffer in this world, even when the sun is shining and the earth is not broken.

"A few days after entering the shelter," David continued, "our case manager told us she had great news; that she had found us a home. Jenna looked so happy; she must have envisioned a home like the only one we had known, one with warmth, comfort and safety. I was skeptical, but didn't let on. But I did hope; I always hoped. We got into our case manager's car and watched as the buildings of Manhattan blurred in the distance. A short time later, we pulled up in front of a bunch of row houses. 'We're here,' our case manager said. I waited for our new family to come out and greet us, but no one appeared. Jenna and I just sat in the car unmoving. 'Which one?' I asked her. She told me it was the white house with black shutters. I looked up at our new home. It was old with neglect. The window ledges had chipped paint and the black shutters were faded from the sun. The front porch was large and covered with the green turf of miniature golf courses. It held six or seven folding lawn chairs and one of those Little Tykes children's toy cars. Yet that day, no one was outside; no one was eager to meet their new son or daughter. Then again, we were just their foster kids; we weren't their real ones. I decided right then not ever to allow myself to get too close to them, or to anyone ever again. Jenna was my only focus. My job from that day forward was only to protect her.

"Finally, our case manager came around and opened up my car door, the one closest to the curb. 'Come on,' she said. I looked at her with apprehension as I slowly climbed out of the car and waited for Jenna. The case manager had already opened the trunk and was readying our things: the two suitcases that contained all we had left of our childhood. I grabbed them and led the way, assuring Jenna that all would be okay, that we just needed to stick together. I could feel Jenna's breath from behind me; she stayed so close. The main front door was open and just a metal and screen door covered the entry. Through the screen, I could see the shadows of a room overcrowded with furniture and children's toys. I could hear voices echo from deep within the house.

"'I said no!' one yelled.

"'Why?' a child asked. Our case manager rang the doorbell.

"'Who is it?' another voice asked.

"'Just go get it!' the first voice yelled.

"A small boy came to the door. He must have been only four or five. He yelled to his mom from afar; announcing the strangers, his foster siblings, at the door. A large woman with bleached hair came to the door carrying a toddler on her right hip. She warmly welcomed us as she unlocked and opened the screen door with her free hand and led us into the main room. I just stood there by the door unsure of moving, Jenna by my side.

"'Well, come on in,' the woman said. 'I won't bite.'

"I wasn't so sure, but eventually let go of the suitcases, allowing them to rest on the floor while gently placing my hand on Jenna's. I guided her slowly to the large rust-colored sofa where we both sat, silently and with eyes wide with fear and uncertainty. We listened while the two women talked and looked over papers. And then our case manager left. I never bothered to learn her name.

"'Well,' the large blonde woman said, 'grab your things and I'll show you to your new room. Claire should be home from school soon.'

"'Who's Claire?' Jenna asked.

"'Claire's your foster sister,' she said. 'She'll be glad to have some company in that big old room.'

"Then we followed her upstairs and to the attic of the white house with the faded black shutters.

"'Welcome to your new home,' she said smiling.

"And then she left us in a large attic room with several old mattresses, all covered with sleeping bags. Two dressers were wedged against the wall between the two parts of the ceiling that slanted down. The floors, made of old, worn wood, were partially covered with a musty-smelling shaggy green rug. I turned to ask the woman a question, but she had gone. And that was pretty much the story at her house. Other than mealtime, or passing through the house, we never really saw her. She was busy with her other kids, her real kids as she called them. We fake kids were more like an oversight, kept upstairs in the attic at night; outside and free during the day."

"David," I said, "I'm so sorry. You and Jenna must have felt so lonely."

"No, we never felt lonely; we had each other. And in a way, we adopted Claire. The three of us considered ourselves a family; we stuck together."

Claire. I remembered what Lance had said. How he thought that Claire had killed Leah. Should I tell David? How close was he to her? And why should I believe anything that Lance told me; after all, he had lied to me

173

about other things, about Leah. I decided to ask instead of tell.

"David, tell me about Claire. What was she like when you first met her?"

"She was hard," he said. "That first day when we heard the school bus roll up the street, Jenna and I peered out of the window hoping to get a glance of the other kids. Sure enough we saw two blonde kids running with lunch boxes toward our house; the real kids. Not long after, we saw another girl, our age, walking alone and with her long blonde hair covering her face; the other foster kid. When she entered the room she just said, 'Who are you?'

"I said, 'David, and this is Jenna.'

"'This is my bed,' she said back. She sat down on the largest of the four mattresses and pulled out a cigarette. I mean, here she was ten or eleven years old and she was bossy, mean, and smoking; it was love at first sight for me. I thought I saw a girl who had it all so under control that nobody could touch her. I smiled and claimed the bed on the other side of the room, and Jenna the one next to me. And that's how my obsessions began: one with Claire, another with protecting Jenna, and finally an obsession with not getting too close to others. I guess it all started in those first moments of loss."

The banging on the door had stopped. Everything was silent.

"I love you," I said.

"I love you too," he repeated.

"I'm sorry that happened to you," I said.

"Sometimes I wonder how it would have all turned out if Jenna and I were given a different path. But then I think that I am who I'm supposed to be, that all of that and what happened after brought me to this very moment...brought me to you and to Hope."

I reached across Hope and lay my hand on top of his. I don't think I could have loved him more than at that moment.

"Enough of my story," he said. "Now it's your turn. I want to know everything about you Sarah."

"Okay," I agreed. "But later. Right now I just want to think about your words, to let them circulate through me as I try and internalize the events and emotions you experienced. I know it sounds strange, but for just a while I want to feel your feelings." He leaned over and kissed me. His soft lips pressed gently against mine and for a brief moment I could feel him; all of him. It was as if his deepest thoughts and fears became a part of me and we were one. My God, I loved him. I loved him so much that it scared me.

With his face positioned over mine, he gave me a smile. I looked into his beautiful face and felt his long hair tickle the sides of my cheeks. I smiled back. He silently got up and, taking his rifle, walked back toward the door and stood guard. He may have grown up from the little boy in the foster home, but he would never grow away from his feeling that he needed to protect the people in his life, and now his people were Hope and me. Suddenly feeling incredibly safe, I closed my eyes to sleep. I tried to imagine David as a ten-year-old boy. I wondered how tall he was, how long his hair was, how his face moved when he smiled. I tried to imagine what he looked like before his innocence was stolen away. And then words came to me, without warning this time: "And at that hour there was a great earthquake, and a tenth of the city fell." And then the earth began to shake.

26

Cars

"David!" I screamed. Hope, jolted into our violent reality, immediately began to cry. I instinctively scooped her into my arms and nestled her against my breast. David attempted to run over to us. The building shook and shook, and it was all David could do not to be jettisoned off the side of the building. Pieces of earth, trees and other debris began raining on us. I sheltered Hope as best as I could as her wails were silenced by the defining roar of the winds. Closing my eyes, I hunched over her and waited for it to stop. And finally it did. Everything became eerily silent and I allowed myself to rise from my crouched position. Hope began to settle into mild whimpers as she had exhausted herself to the threshold of sleep. I became conscious of my body; it felt unscathed by the violence. Next, I looked for

David. I could see him lying on his side not far from the door. He lifted his head and called out to me.

"Sarah," he said. "Are you and Hope okay?"

"Yes, we're both fine. You?"

"I'm okay," he replied.

I placed my hands on my eyes and rubbed in both the weariness and gratefulness. We were still alive. Again I looked up at David. He was in the process of standing, his gun at his side, when I noticed the door. The violent shaking had dislodged its iron barrier.

Before I could yell a warning, two men stepped out onto our roof with their guns drawn. One lifted his weapon toward David and shots rang out. I watched as one man fell to the ground, and the other went running back into the building. David again readied his rifle waiting for more intruders, but no more came, at least for now. He lifted the man's body and threw it back into the belly of the building, and then reclosed and bolted the door. As he began his short trek over to me, the earth again began to shake. He fell next to me and Hope and covered us both with his arms. We waited as a second round of movement filled the earth. The building whimpered under the pressure and I worried that it would come crashing down with us intact. The skies lit up and seemed to split into two with deafening thunder. Under its power, the earth seemed frightened, responding with its own trembling. David and I hunched over our daughter who was still passed out from the trauma of the first round. Finally, it subsided and we let our breath ease. Our rooftop sanctuary now threatened danger. Large cracks and crevices had broken out along the top and it was obvious that the building would soon collapse.

"We've got to get off of here and out of this building," I said.

J.E.Byrne

David looked at me and Hope contemplating our vulnerable conditions.

"I can do it," I said. "You carry Hope."

He looked concerned, but nodded.

"David," I added with confidence. "I need my gun. It's in the pocket of the sweatshirt I was wearing." I watched as he reached into his own pocket and handed it to me. My eyes met his in the acknowledgment of a new society clothed in violence.

"You sure you can make it?" he asked.

I nodded. *Even if I couldn't,* I thought, *I'd make sure that they both did.* We had no other choice. Quickly we gathered the remaining food, water, and supplies that hadn't fallen out of reach into the newly formed crevices, and stuffed them into our packs. As fast as possible we approached the door. He handed me Hope while he went to open and defend its barrier. David looked at me for confirmation to proceed. I lifted my head and gave him the go. He lifted his weapon as he unbolted the door. He entered the portal behind his rifle.

"Clear," he yelled as he placed his rifle strap around his right shoulder and then lifted Hope from my arms and into his.

"I'll go first," I said. I held my gun in my right hand, remembering who I was after the safe house and before giving birth. I was young, strong, and armed; I was a survivor. I began running down the steps of the building. At first I felt okay, but after the first few floors, I began to feel a pulling in my lower half, and there was a damp and sticky presence between my thighs. Just as I was about to stop and check, a person from below appeared and began shooting. I aimed my gun and fired at her; at least I thought it was a her. Two or three others ran out from hiding. David and I crouched down on the stairs as they began to shoot at us. I

178

raised my gun and tried to shoot back, but they had better cover than we did. The railings on the stairs left us vulnerable. *This is it* I thought; *not a bang but a whimper.* It felt so disappointing.

But then again the earth began to shake, even harder this time, knocking us over and down the stairs. Hope was safely nestled inside of David's soft coat and I was able to fall onto my knees. When the shaking stopped, I looked down to see our attackers crushed underneath a ceiling that had collapsed onto them. Relieved that we were still alive, I got up and again began running down the stairs with David and Hope following. As we approached the next floor, I heard a person's cries.

"Please help me," he said. "Please, please help me."

I looked toward the voice. It was one of the people who had been shooting at us. He was pinned under heavy wood and dry wall, and it was obvious that he would never be released from its weight. I walked over to the suffering man, placed my gun next to his temple, and fired a single shot. His suffering was over. I looked up to see David staring at me. He hadn't seen this me before, but it was who I had become. We continued down the rest of the stairs until we reached the door to the outside. It was blocked with tons of rubble. David and I looked at each other with the realization that we were prisoners inside of what was once our sanctuary. David handed me Hope. I sat down and held her as she began to fuss. I guided her to my breast where she took comfort in feeding. I watched as David took off to inspect the rest of the ground floor.

"Over here!" he yelled. "There's an opening over here!"

Excitedly, I went to get up. But upon my first effort I felt a gushing of warmth come out of my body. I knew it wasn't good. I looked down at the small amount of leg that was exposed between my black sweats and my boots. It was painted with blood. I looked up at David who had already seen.

"Oh my God," he said. He came over and scooped me up from the ground. He carried me out of the crumbling building and outside onto the vulnerable earth. The ground was filled with crevices and chasms, and David carefully maneuvered his footing while carrying me and Hope.

"David," I said. "Please. Just put me down. It's no use. I can't go on. You take Hope and meet the others in Indianapolis. You can make it; I know you can make it."

"No," he said. "I already told you that I would never leave you again."

"But this time I want you to go. I want you to save our daughter…please."

"No," he insisted. "I'll think of something." He strained with my weight as he maneuvered around the broken earth. After ten minutes of very little progress, he relented and lowered me to the ground. I felt weak from losing so much blood. Hope began to cry. I nestled her to my breast. David sat down next to me.

"God, please save my family," I heard him say.

And then we felt the earth move again and saw bright lights that blinded our eyes. But this time it wasn't only an earthquake and sky-splitting lightening; this time it was also the approaching high beams of a car. It pulled up next to us. The door swung open, and a voice commanded us, "Get in."

27

Rescued

I looked helplessly up at David as he crawled onto
his knees, leaned down, and bundled me up. With Hope in
my arms, I felt him place me into the back seat of the car.
He then jumped in next to me and slammed the door shut.
And then the strange car, with my family inside, zoomed
away from the disintegrating earth. We sat silently for a few
moments until the driver found the way back to route 70.
The roadway was heavily damaged and the car had to
navigate its labyrinth. I didn't want to distract the driver, but
at the same time I needed to know if we were saved or
doomed. David, on the other hand, didn't seem to care
about the driver of the car; he was focused only on me.

I watched as he gently placed Hope on the seat next
to him and then grabbed his backpack. He ripped open the

zipper and pulled out rags and bandages, and then he proceeded to undo my many layers of clothes.

"Sarah," he whispered as he saw the damage. I figured his reaction didn't indicate good news.

"I'll be okay," I whispered. But I could feel the weakness creeping in. I willed myself to keep my eyes open, to stay awake.

David took some of the water bottles and poured them onto my legs, trying to wipe away the blood. Next he grabbed his collection of bandages and pressed then into a tight mass.

"I'm sorry Sarah," he said, "this is going to hurt."

I tried to contain my cry as he endeavored to save my hemorrhaging body, pressing hard to stop the bleeding. I kept my eyes focused on his, tears streaming from both of our cheeks. Hope began to whimper. I watched as he took his left hand and bundled her up, laying her small body gently on my chest. I nestled her close to me wondering if these would be the last moments that I would know her on this earth. There we were. My family. The three of us huddled in the back seat of a stranger's car, each fighting for life: one suckling it, one clinging to it, and another vigorously fighting for it. I could feel the thrashing of the vehicle as it avoided the damaged areas of the roadway. I could feel David's force upon me as he willed my body to stop bleeding, and I could feel the warmth and gentle tug of Hope at my breast. Time passed, and eventually I fell asleep.

When I next awoke, I could see David still next to me, still looking into my eyes. Upon seeing mine opened, he smiled.

"Did it stop?" I asked him.

"Yes," he said. "It stopped."

"Thank you," I whispered. I saw Hope safely resting in his arms. I smiled and allowed myself to fall back asleep. The next time I awoke, I again looked up into someone's eyes, but they were not David's. Startled, I went to sit up when the stranger calmed me.

"Sarah, it's me," the voice said. I knew that voice. I looked again.

"Jack!" I said as my face lit up into a thousand suns, "Oh Jack!" I lifted my arms to him and he leaned over and gently gave me a hug.

"Sarah," he said. "I'm glad you're so happy to see me."

"Of course I am, Jack. I'm sorry I left you. Please know how very sorry I am."

"I do," he said. "But I knew you'd be back. I always knew."

"Yes, you did," I answered.

"I didn't know you had a license," David chimed in from the driver's seat. I could see that they had traded places. I wondered how long we had been on the road.

"Are you complaining?" Jack kidded.

"No buddy, I'm definitely not," David answered. "Thanks for rescuing us."

"You're welcome," Jack said with a pleased grin.

I looked up into his face. He had grown so much in the months I had been away. The apocalypse had aged us all, even children. Jack was a man. His voice had changed and I could see the leanness of manhood in his cheeks.

"How did you find us?" I asked him.

"I just knew," he said with a telling look.

"Of course you did," I replied. Jack's gift of prophecy no longer surprised me, but the car did. "Where did you find a working car?" I added to my list of questions.

J.E.Byrne

"I'll tell you everything Sarah, but first, can I hold her?"

I saw his eyes fixed on Hope. I gently lifted her from my chest and offered her to him. Jack's smile broadened as he accepted Hope, and she quickly nestled into his embrace.

"She's beautiful," he said.

"I didn't know you liked babies," I joked.

"I like *her*," he said. "She's a miracle, Sarah."

"Yes, she is," I added.

"David told me all about her while you were sleeping. You were really brave, Sarah."

"Thanks, Jack."

"Is it okay that I call you my sister?" he asked. "I've just always seen you as my big sister."

"Of course," I whispered. Jack was my second chance of being a good big sister, since I had failed so epically with Ben. "That makes you Hope's uncle, you know," I said.

"Uncle Jack," he said aloud. "I like it. Look, she's staring at me. I think she knows me," he said.

I remained quiet for a while and just watched him enjoying Hope. He spoke to her and she seemed to respond to all of his words. I marveled at the bond that was being forever cemented by these two innocent victims of the earth's fall. I loved them both more than just as a child and brother, I loved them as equals, as a part of everything who I was and had become. It was as though the fires of the end had baptized David, Hope, Jack and me as one.

"She's starting to cry," Jack said. He handed Hope back to me. I quickly quieted her at my breast while Jack looked away a little embarrassed; he was still a twelve-year-old adolescent after all.

"You ready to tell me about that car?" I asked.

184

"Yeah," he said excitedly. "After David left, we waited, as agreed, for a few days. I didn't want to leave, but I had promised him."

"I'm right here!" David said.

"Yeah, I promised you," Jack said tapping David on the shoulder. "Anyway, we took off onto route 70 toward Indianapolis, our planned meeting place," he said looking at me while keeping his hand on David's shoulder.

"Is everyone okay?" I interrupted. "Is the whole group still together?"

"Yes, everyone is fine and excited to see you and David."

"How do they know that we're coming?"

"I assured the others that I had seen it in a dream. That I knew where to find you and that I would bring you both back. Sarah," he added as if he sensed my worry, "they knew I'd find you. They trusted me."

"But why didn't anyone come with you Jack?"
Even though he looked like a young man, I thought, *he was just a boy. Why hadn't Ruth come, or Josh?*

And as if he picked up my thoughts, Jack said, "Sarah, I'm not a child anymore. I'm not allowed to be. A few nights ago, I dreamt of you. I saw myself rescuing you. I clearly saw where to go and how to get there. I saw you, and David, and Hope. I told the others. I told them I needed to go. They trusted me. They knew that I would find you and bring you back. End of story."

I looked again into his face. I was wrong; he was a man. I guess the crucible of the end refined us all. I smiled at him. He smiled back.

"So tell me where the car came in?" I asked.

"Two days after David left, we hit the road. We walked past a car dealership. We went to check out the cars, to see if anything was left behind, but quickly discovered that people were living in them. We began to scatter, afraid of our discovery. But a woman named Naomi called out to us. She assured us that we were in no danger. Outnumbered, we allowed ourselves to approach their group. They had formed some type of community; they weren't fighting or eating each other; they were living together, kind of like we were."

"That's reassuring," I said as the car swerved to avoid an obstacle on the earthquake damaged road.

"Yes, it was," Jack continued. "And after talking with them, we discovered that many of them, too, had seen visions of The Mountain, and so were also headed toward Colorado. We stayed with them for a while. We shared stories; I told them about you and David, and how we were planning to meet up with you in Indianapolis. They were particularly interested whenever we spoke of you. I felt like maybe, in a strange way, they had heard about you before. Then, one night, I had a dream of your rescue. In it, I saw you and David, and your location on top of a large brick building that was across from a hospital. I saw that you had given birth, and that your building was crumbling and being attacked, and that you were in danger. I woke up panicked and determined to find you. I met with our group; I told them I was going to look for you, that I had been told in a dream to rescue you. The new people, the ones we were staying with, all looked at each other; it was as if they had a secret. And they did; they had a car that worked. When they heard my account of the dream, they gave me their one working car, probably the only working car in the entire world, to use in rescuing you. They were determined that you be saved. They got out a map and showed me, based upon my description in the dream, where exactly to go to find you. So I took the car and drove to the place where they had directed me, the same one that I had seen in the dream.

And as the earth was shaking you out of the building, I pulled up right in front and saw you on the ground."

"How did you know how to drive?" David asked.

"Four wheelers. Lots of time on four wheelers; it's the same thing."

"Really?" I asked.

"Yeah, especially when dodging earthquakes," he said.

"And no one else wanted to accompany you on your joy ride?" David asked.

"They weren't supposed to," Jack said. "I mean, I know it sounds crazy, but in my dream it was only me. I didn't need anyone else to be in danger."

"And did your dream tell us where to go next?" I asked.

"Of course it did," he said. "We are headed back to their camp. The others will meet us there."

"How close are we?" I asked. I suddenly felt so excited to see the other members of my family: Ruth, Jared and Britney, Josh, Sam and his family; I couldn't wait for our reunion.

David spoke. "Based on the directions you gave me, we've got to be almost there."

"How's the gas situation?" Jack asked. "I think we used all of the extra containers that were in the trunk."

"As far as I can tell," David said, "we should have run out an hour ago."

And just as his words left his lips, we did run out of gas. The car stopped in what appeared to be the heart of an empty downtown Indianapolis. And as soon as the car stopped, we could feel the danger.

28

Naomi

For a few minutes, we all remained silent. How should we exit the car? Who was going to carry me? Why hadn't we come up with a plan before? And then, before we could take action, we saw shadows approaching. David made sure the locks were thrown down and I pressed Hope so tightly to my chest that she let out a small cry.

"What are we going to do?" I asked. I could see hands at the doors; hear the sounds of clicking as fingers tried to open the latches. My heart began to race as David turned around and looked helplessly at us in the back seat.

"Open the door," Jack commanded.

"Are you crazy?" I asked.

"No, really," he said as he unlocked his door and went to grab the handle.

"Jack, stop!" I yelled. But it was too late. He had opened his door and the people outside had already begun placing their hands on him. I watched in horror as two of them stuck their heads through the opened door and peered at me and Hope lying in the back seat, featured in the car's upper light.

"It's her," one of them said. David quickly climbed over the seat and formed a barrier between me and the intruders.

"No David," Jack's voice said from outside the car. "It's okay, these people are safe; they are good. They're the ones who sent me to rescue you."

David turned and looked at the people huddled around the opened door. I lowered my head so that I, too, could see their faces. I saw a woman, not much older than I, smiling at me. She didn't look like the walking dead that I had encountered so many times before; she looked beautiful and inspired and best of all, she looked like she wanted to help me, not eat me.

"David," I said, "It is okay. They're not going to hurt us." I watched as he slowly turned back toward them and spoke.

"We need help," he said. "Sarah can't walk."

The people backed away and I could hear a rattling noise as I saw Jack approach with a shopping cart. "Sarah can ride in here," he said. "We can push her in this cart."

David nodded and then proceeded to lift me and Hope out of the protection of the car, and into the raw air of the night. As he placed my weakened body into the cart, I alerted to new smells and senses. The sky had grown somewhat lighter after the quakes. It held a greenish hue, much like after the first explosion all those many months ago. I could see the silhouettes and even the faces of seven or eight people surrounding us. The air smelled like sulfur and felt unnatural and unstable. While it was still cool from the lack of natural light, the quakes seemed to have stolen

189

some of the chill. As I lay back in the shopping cart, I allowed myself to relax. I had no control over the situation; I had no control over anything anymore. I wondered if I ever really did, even in my old life. I would just have to concede; I would have to trust. I reached up and grabbed David's hand. He squeezed it hard, letting me know that he was there for me. No matter what happened next, he was going to experience it with me.

I watched as he and Jack began pushing me and Hope behind the people who were leading us. Jack called to them and knew most by name. As we rolled along, some would circle around, peering inside the cart, wanting to get a glimpse of Hope and me. I felt self-conscious and somewhat awkward.

"Jack," I asked, "What's going on?"

"These are the people I told you about. They talked about you as if they knew you; they gave me the car to go find you."

"But *how* do they know her?" David asked.

"I'm not sure," Jack said. "When I told them about you, before I left, and how I had dreamt of your danger, they sent me quickly off to find you. We didn't have time to talk of it then. But we can ask them later, after we get safely off of the road."

David took over pushing the cart, while Jack navigated behind the others. The gradually brightening skies shaved off the bits of claustrophobic darkness from the previous months. It felt freeing to catch glimpses of roads, buildings, signs, and even of other people. We had to pilot ourselves off a clover leaf of partially destroyed highways and upturned grassy strips until we found our way to a large structure. As we approached, I could see a large sign: Frank's Subaru. I couldn't help but chuckle at the raw irony. The sanctuary of our visionaries wasn't some poignantly

symbolic code as one might expect; or even a Mercedes or
Range Rover dealership; it was good old Frank's Subaru.
And as we entered its large lot, the macadam remarkably
untouched by the quake, I saw more people: the group Jack
had spoken of. These were the ones, who besides us, had
gathered in their shared dream of The Mountain. Others
who were headed west to Colorado…to Mt. Elbert. Others
who had huddled in safety and community at a simple car
dealership in Indianapolis.

"Sarah!" a little girl said as if she were a long lost
friend. "Over here! We made a place for you." I watched as
a woman, who must have been her mother or older sister,
quieted her while motioning us toward them. David, also
relenting to trust, pushed us over to where they were
standing. A light gray Subaru was waiting, its hatch open
and welcoming. I smiled. It only made sense that I would be
offered refuge in a Subaru, the same car I had for years
shared with my mom, dad, and Ben. David gently carried
me from the cart and placed me in the large, flat space in
back of the car. He lifted Hope and nestled her small body
in the strength of his long arms. I adjusted myself so that I
could sit up and see all that was happening around us.

"I can't thank all of you enough," I heard David say
to the twenty or so people gathered. "Jack says that you
gave him your only working car so that he could rescue us.
And then you helped us safely bring Sarah and Hope here.
Thanks very much."

A tall, authoritative-looking woman walked forward
and lifted her hand. David accepted her offer and shifting
Hope onto his left side, met her hand in greeting.

"My name is Naomi. Welcome to our camp."

"How long have you been here?" he asked.

"Not long," she responded. "A couple of weeks."

"Why are you here?" he asked.

"We've been waiting for you," she said.

With her words I felt a chill run throughout my body, and it gave Hope a slight quiver.

"Why have you been waiting for *us*?" I chimed in from behind David. I watched as he moved aside to reveal me to the woman. "How is it that you know us?"

"I'm sorry, Sarah," she said. "I figured that you already knew who you were."

"Who am I?" I asked.

Naomi laughed at my words; it made me feel silly and confused.

"What's so funny?" I questioned as I looked up into her face. With reddish hair and fair skin, she looked a bit like my mom, only stronger in both stature and affect.

"You don't even know who you are," she said.

"Who do you think I am?" I asked.

"You're the one who's going to change everything," she said.

"Why do people keep saying that?" I responded. "People really need to stop saying that."

"They can't," she replied. "The truth can't be kept silent."

"What truth?" David asked.

"That Sarah is the one to lead us," she said.

"I've never led anyone to anything good," I said under my breath.

David walked over with Hope still in his arms, and I gratefully accepted her as not only my own, but also as a way to end the odd conversation with the woman named Naomi. She smiled at me as I held Hope against my body to keep her feeling warm and secure.

"Right now it's time for you to get some rest," Naomi said. "We can talk more later."

Yeah, doubt it, I thought.

192

Hollow Land

But I did welcome the opportunity to lie down in the belly of the large car. With the back seats flattened, it was almost the size of my bed at home. *Home*, I thought, trying to visualize my life before, my room with the pink walls and little girl canopy bed; what was home now? Better yet, where was home now?

"You okay?" David asked as he climbed in next to me and lay down.

"I'm not sure," I answered. "People keep saying the strangest things."

He wrapped me and Hope in his long and strong arms as I continued my whining, "Like I'm supposed to be this leader or something. That I'm supposed to change things."

"Well, I know I'd follow you anywhere," he said as he turned his head and kissed me softly on the lips. His kiss stirred me and I responded, allowing our lips to linger. I didn't really know how long we would have to wait for my body to heal before we could be together the first time, as husband and wife, but I hoped it wouldn't be too much longer.

"I love you," he whispered in my ear before laying his head back flat and quickly succumbing to his fatigue.

"I love you, too," I said to the night air as I closed my eyes and willed sleep. I wanted nothing more than to drown out my rambling thoughts and fears. But sleep wouldn't come, and I found myself mulling over the words spoken first by Leah at the rest stop many months ago, then by Jake after he rescued me from the wild dogs, and now from this woman Naomi as she welcomed me into her group of twenty or so survivors...*you're the one who's going to change everything.* It was almost ludicrous. Not only did I not have the power to change anything, I didn't even know what needed to be changed. I mean, it would be great if we could all be rescued from this dying world, from this time of danger, but come on; other than finding a celestial version of Mount Elbert, what chance did we all have of that? Maybe that was it. Maybe I was supposed to just tell them the name of The Mountain and give them directions, or maybe they were just supposed to follow us. But I wasn't even sure Mt. Elbert was the right one. Sam Eirmann was the one who had that vision. Sam and Jack were the ones who should be leading the survivors. *I can't do it*, I thought. I have a newborn baby to take care of and a new husband I'm longing to devour. *I won't do it; whatever it is they think I should do, I won't.* And then thankfully with my decision made, I joined both David and Hope in slumber.

Later, I awoke to Hope's hungry cries.

"Shhh," I tried to comfort her before she awakened David who was still sleeping soundly by my side. I nestled her against my chest as I turned over to look at him. I remembered watching him sleep months ago, before I left the group, before I even knew that I was pregnant with Hope. It was when I had fallen ill. David had stayed by my side while I had drifted in and out of consciousness. I remember one time, awakening to him sleeping at my side, much like now, and yet also so different. At that time, he had looked worn and unkempt just like now; yet then he was still chained to his past, and I to mine. Ironically, although we were now chained to our grim life circumstances with the end of the world and all, we were truly free, and in that freedom finally connected in a way that was right and beautiful. I looked at his long, dark hair that he now kept pulled back and away from his face, the way his cheekbones gave strength to his masculinity, and his dark skin that seemed to give him toughness within his handsome features. He must have felt me observing him as he slowly opened his eyes and looked up at me.

"Hi," he said.

"Hi."

"How are you feeling?" he asked.

"Good," I said. And I did. It had been less than a week since I gave birth to Hope, and only hours or days since I had almost bled to death during our escape from the earthquake, yet I felt relatively strong. There was a knocking on our back hatch.

"Yeah, we're awake," David said. The hatch opened and revealed two young children, probably nine or ten years old, standing outside holding a platter full of food. My eyes alerted because for the first time since giving birth, I was famished.

David reached out and accepted the platter from the children with warm thanks. We both sat up with our backs against the upright front seats. He set the large platter on his lap, and I nestled a sleeping Hope in between the two of us. The platter held three apples, and I mean real apples. They were shriveled and dry, but fruit that wasn't overly processed was a gift in any form. Also on the plate were some pieces of tuna or chicken, probably generously shared from someone else's canned supply. I recognized that these people were offering us the best that they had and I greatly appreciated it. David and I both ate well and I felt thoroughly full and satisfied in many ways. I was ready to find Jack and head to the raceway.

"I'm ready," I said to David.

"Ready for what?" He laughed. "Haven't you had enough?"

"Ready to find Jack and get out of here...ready to find Ruth and the others. Jack said it's probably only six or seven miles away," I added.

"Sarah," David said while meeting my eyes, "there's no way you can walk six miles yet; you need to rest and heal for a while."

"Maybe we can find more gas for the car," I suggested. "We could drive there. We could be there in minutes." How I longed to be reunited with Ruth, Britney, Jared and even the Eirmann's. Although I barely got to know them before I left with Lance, they still represented my life before my failed path, and meeting up with them again felt like redemption.

"Okay," David smiled as he leaned over and kissed me, "I'll see what I can find out." He gently lifted the covers so as not to stir Hope, and then he exited the car and walked away to discuss our departure with the others.

Alone with Hope, a full stomach and a healing body, I began to allow myself to dream. Not a fantasy dream, but a hopeful one. I imagined my family: David, Hope, Jack, me and the others all reaching Mt. Elbert. I allowed myself to see us reaching its top, celebrating in its promise of sunlight, green grass, fresh food. Relaxing in its promise of sanctuary and freedom from the dark. I looked down at Hope and smiled, imagining her growing up with Jack as her big brother, pushing her on the swings, teaching her how to talk about all the things we used to value before the explosion took it all away.

"Sarah." David's words startled me from my thoughts.

"Are we good to go?" I asked, invigorated by my recent thoughts and hopes.

"Yes," he said. "Naomi already refueled the car."

"Did you find Jack?" I asked.

"No," David said. "He left during the night to get word back to the others."

"What?" I said even though I had totally heard him. "But we only just found him," I added under my breath.

"He'll be alright," David said. "He probably wanted to let them know that we were safe, and that we were coming."

I understood. Young Jack was a man in his wisdom.

"There's more," David said.

"What is it?" I asked, not sure that I wanted to hear any more news.

"The people here, they want to come with us. They want you to lead them."

"Did you just explain to them that the destination is Mt. Elbert in Colorado and so all they have to do is walk straight away on route 70 and then they will get there? They don't need me!"

"Yes, I told them," he said. "But Naomi is convinced that you are essential to getting there. And look, Sarah, is it really so bad if they travel with us? I mean look at how they've helped us, and Naomi told me that they could aid in finding future provisions."

"You mean if there are future provisions," I added.

"True," he said. "But if there aren't, we're all screwed anyway, aren't we?"

"I guess," I said. "How will they get there? I thought there was only one working car."

"There is," he said. "And they are giving it to us. They will follow on foot to the raceway and meet us there."

"David, I don't know; this whole thing is kind of creeping me out. They are convinced that I'm someone I'm not."

"Don't be so sure," he said.

"Oh great, did Naomi get to you too?"

David came by me and laid his hand on my calf. "Naomi didn't try and convince me to do anything," he said.

197

"It's just that nothing surprises me anymore, especially when it has to do with you."

I smiled back at him.

"I love you, you know," he said.

"Yes," I replied with a relenting smile, "and I love you, too."

"Well then," he said, "the people here are packed and ready, let's not disappoint."

So I gently scooped up our daughter and crawled out of the car. David gathered the blankets and empty platter and bundled them in his arms to return to Naomi. As I climbed outside of the car, I could see that the twenty or so in Naomi's group were sitting by their nomadic bundles, ready to make the journey behind us. In the middle of the lot, the lone working car, perhaps the only one on the entire globe sat waiting for David, Hope and me. I felt like a spoiled celebrity as I looked around and felt compelled to call out, "I am incredibly grateful to you all for sharing your car at a time when my body is not yet able to walk long distances. The car, however, can hold many more folks than just the three of us. Please send us your young, old, or sick so that they may join us in driving the distance."

I looked over at David who nodded at my action. He grabbed my hand and whispered in my ear, "You see, you were born to lead." I looked up at him and felt myself blushing. Maybe there was more to me than I thought; at least I could hope so.

All was silent for a few minutes before Naomi smiled and walked around encouraging certain people to join us for the short drive. And within minutes, David, Hope, and I were joined by four small kids, a man whose ankle was injured during the quakes, and one old woman who seemed weakened by the struggle to live.

"Follow 16th street to Brickyard Crossing," Naomi called out to David. "Stop at the intersection; they'll meet you there. It's on a golf course."

We motored away from the car lot and toward the Indianapolis Speedway. *Here we come,* I thought with pangs of excitement. *Here we come!*

29

Job

David gently pressed the pedal and our car began its short journey to the Raceway. Even though it was little more than six or seven miles away, we had to travel slowly and carefully along the earthquake damaged road. I figured it would take us twenty or thirty minutes to get there, so the rest of the group would probably not be too far behind. I considered our meeting place, a golf course in front of a public raceway. *I always hated golf,* I thought. *And why would we meet in such a public place? Hadn't we learned to avoid anywhere that could attract others?*

Realizing there wasn't much I could do about it except hold tightly onto Hope while the car tossed and turned through the dimpled terrain, I decided to take notice of my travelling partners. In the front seat were David, the old woman, and the injured man who held a small child on his lap. Wedged on both sides of me were the children, two on my left and one on my right.

"Can I touch her?" the small girl on my right asked breaking me out of my thoughts.

"Of course," I told her. "Her name is Hope."

"We know her name," a boy to my left said. "We know Hope, and you Sarah, and David, and Jack."

"Really," I said. "And to think I don't know any of your names. Now that doesn't sound fair, does it?" I teased.

The small boy laughed and responded, "My name is Jacob, and this is Sophie, and she is Megan." He pointed to the young girl who was now gently brushing Hope's forehead.

I looked at the children sitting along my two sides. They were so young; I wondered how much they could even still remember about their lives before the explosion.

"How old are you Jacob?" I asked.

"Seven," he said. "And Sophie and Megan are six."

"Sarah," I heard a worn and shaky voice rise up from the front seat. "My name is Norah, and next to me are Robert and Caitlin." Robert nodded, but did not speak. The small child on his lap appeared to have fallen asleep.

"Nice to meet all of you," I said. The car took a heavy swerve to the left and we all pressed upon each other. Hope began to cry, and I brought her close and whispered comforting words by her soft cheek.

"Sorry," David said as he slowed to a crawl and straightened the wheel. "The conditions of the road seem to be deteriorating." Hope's cries grew louder, and I could tell the children were frightened. I could feel their small bodies snuggling closer to me, and Megan's hand moved away from Hope.

"It's okay children," Norah said from the front seat. "Even though things sometimes seem scary, we are never truly left unprotected," she said.

"What do you mean?" asked Jacob.

A questioner, I thought. I already really liked this kid.

"Well," she said, "why don't I tell you a story about a man who was met with all kinds of scary trouble and yet was completely restored in the end?"

"What's restored?" asked Jacob

"That means he was okay," she answered him.

"Yes!" both he and Sophie shouted on my left, and a still frightened Megan whispered at my right. I could tell by their excitement and the way it comforted them that this was not the first time Norah had told them a story. I'm guessing that storytelling was the gift she carried to her small post-apocalyptic community. Of course I loved stories too, so I was in.

"Okay," Norah began. "This story is about a man named Job."

"That's a weird name," Jacob commented.

"Well, I guess it is," said Norah. "But his story proves that even if he did have a weird name, he was very brave." And so she began.

"As I said, Job was considered a brave and wise man. Wise means that he understood things that most people could not. So, brave and wise Job lived a very good life. He was rich and happy, and had a wife, and many sons and daughters.

"One day, a very bad man (so bad that sometimes I will even call him evil), went to see God, who was Job's Creator. That meant that God was the one who made Job.

Hollow Land

The bad man said mean and untrue things about Job. He told God that Job only loved him because God had given Job a life that was easy and filled with many good things. Well, God told the evil man that this was not true; that Job loved him because Job understood that He, God, was worthy of his love. What God meant was that His relationship with Job had nothing to do with things...it was based on trust and respect and love."

I looked down at Hope's face as she slept. I thought about how much I loved her, that I would do anything for her. Love wasn't dependent upon circumstances, or at least it shouldn't be. Then again, I was so angry with God after my father died. I guess I still was angry with him. Look at all that had happened. Consider all of the pain and suffering that we all were enduring. Why should I still love God, let alone believe in him? My thoughts drifted as Norah's words swooped me back into Job's troubles.

"Well, the bad man told God that he was wrong, that if Job were to lose his good life, that he would no longer want to be God's friend. God, knowing Job's heart and knowing this was untrue, gave the evil man dominion over Job's life. That meant that God allowed the man to make Job's life very difficult. So the evil man brought trouble to Job. He destroyed Job's home, his family, and his wealth. But still Job loved his Creator, God. When Job's wife told him to curse God, Job asked her, 'Should we only accept the good things from God and not the bad?' Job trusted God, even in the worst of times. The evil man did not understand and sent disease to Job. Job became very sick and troubled and he asked God for help, but God did not seem to answer him.

"After some time, Job had lost everything except his very life. Three of Job's friends came to visit him. They told Job that he must have been very bad to deserve such

203

horrible treatment from God. They told Job that he should admit that he had done many evil things. But Job knew that this was not true. Job knew that he had lived a good life and that he had always tried to honor and please his Creator. He knew that he was not being punished, but was just being called to live amongst difficult circumstances.

"Many people laughed at Job. Some ignored him, and none respected him. Job felt lonely and sad. He called out to God and asked Him why He had forgotten him. He questioned God and why He had allowed such awful things to happen. One day God answered Job. God reminded Job that He, God, was still in control, even in times of darkness. He reminded Job that He, God, was the creator of mankind, the animals, and even the earth, and that He had purpose in all things, both the good and the bad.

"Being a man who loved and trusted his Creator, Job humbled himself before God. He realized that God had never left him; that God would never leave him. He trusted God's power and His love. He knew that God's purposes were bigger and greater than he could ever understand. Job demonstrated that he loved his Creator not for things or circumstances, but because he believed that God was good and worthy of his love. Job admitted to God, 'Surely I spoke of things I did not understand, things too wonderful for me to know.' Ultimately, Job proved the evil man wrong."

"I don't understand the story Miss Norah," said Sophie.

I don't either, I thought.

"We're here," David said. We all peered out of the windows at the darkened landscape, half excited, half afraid of what we were going to discover.

"Over there," Jacob said. "It looks like a sign."

"Nice job Jacob," David replied. He turned off the headlights and continued at a silent crawl as our car crossed the intersection of 16th street and what we assumed was the Brickyard Crossing Golf Course. David stopped the car and threw down the locks. For a moment or two, we all sat in silence; we weren't really sure what to do next.

"Look," whispered Megan. "I see someone coming."

I quickly moved my head toward her window and strained my eyes to see. There was a figure approaching our car, and I knew his build.

"It's Jack!" I said. "David, it's Jack!"

"Don't open the door until we know for sure," David warned. But I knew that it was him. I waited, smiling and anxious for Jack to get closer, for all to see proof. I saw more people with him. My eyes filled with tears as I felt certain that Jack was accompanied by Ruth, Jared, Britney, Sam, Josh, Rachel, and their little baby. My heart swelled with gratefulness that they would soon greet me and David as husband and wife, and Hope as our daughter. When I left them I was broken, and now I was complete. Yes, bad things had happened, really bad things; but somehow these things had connected me to something bigger. I wasn't quite sure who or what it was, but like Norah's Job, I knew that it was bigger than my personal circumstances.

A tapping at David's window startled me.

"It's him," David said. He threw the locks and I felt the car doors opening to the cool air. Norah turned and nodded to the children, assuring them that all was safe. Each exited the car leaving me and Hope alone in the back seat. And before I could ready myself to exit, I felt the warm embrace of someone who loved me. I recognized the thick and wavy red hair of the woman I had once saved. I looked up into her teary eyes, and smiled as she had already begun gently stroking the smooth top of Hope's head.

"She's so beautiful," Ruth said.

"Ruth," was all I could say back. It was then that I realized that home wasn't a place; it was being in community with the people you loved, and even more importantly, the ones who were always willing to forgive. Even though I was in a place I had never before visited; I knew that I was home.

30

Love Realized

Ruth reached over and placed her arms around my shoulders. I remembered the night I had left, the night when she first confronted me with the truth. Ruth told me that I was pregnant, and then let me weep into her arms. And now, all of this time later, her embrace still felt familiar and secure. I allowed myself to forget about the earthquake, the pain of childbirth, the incineration of my friends and family, and the perplexing story of Job, as I melted into her nurturing hug. I didn't ever want her to let go.

"We better leave the car," I heard David say.

"Naomi told us she would hide it after they arrived," Jack replied.

"Would you carry Hope?" I asked Ruth in preparation of my exit from the car.

I watched as her face swelled in the delight of the call for her maternal gifts. I lifted Hope to her arms, and she eagerly swept her up and away from the vehicle. *Amazing, I thought, how we can find moments of joy even within hours of sorrow.* I don't think I'll ever fully understand the mysteries of mankind, but I felt it, too. The man whom I loved, my husband, gently reached in and lifted me from the car. He held me close to his strong chest as he followed the others away from the car and toward the emptiness of the golf course. I felt his steps, even as he tried to minimize each one in an attempt to protect my healing body from any unnecessary jarring. I nestled my head into the base of his neck. His scent was musky and woodsy, and I found it overwhelmingly masculine and utterly desirable.

"Hi, Sarah." I looked to my left and saw Jack by my side. "Over there," he said to David while pointing to the right. The group led us to a large white building at the edge of the golf course. I watched as Jack, Jared, and Sam opened one of the large doors in the front of the structure.

"Go ahead in," Jack said.

"Aren't you all coming?" I asked him.

"Not today," Jack said.

Ruth and Rachel neared my side. Ruth was still holding Hope. "It's your wedding present," Rachel said. "Jack told us that you and David were married."

I opened my mouth to summon more inquiries, but Ruth stopped me. "No more questions," she said. Just follow the path we created and enjoy your time together. Rachel and I will take care of Hope. The rest of the group will all be outside, standing guard, making sure that you and David get to celebrate and honor your newly made vows."

I looked up into David's face as I felt both nervousness and heated excitement. He met my eyes with what appeared to be similar emotions.

"Thank you," he said barely in a whisper, never letting his eyes leave mine. Ruth and Rachel departed and we heard the large doors close us off from everyone. While I had been anxious to catch up with the others and hear their stories, my passion for David blurred those needs. All I wanted now was to be with him, and I mean for the first time really *be* with him.

He carried me off through the narrow path of defunct golf carts until we reached the back of the structure. There, secluded along the back corner, was an area set up for our union. Candles were lit along a large bed made up of soft blankets and pillows for which our group must have searched and sacrificed. The top blanket was white and as we got closer and David gently placed me down, I could see was covered with silky petals from an artificial red rose. To the left was a large tub of water, and next to it was soap, two white towels, toothpaste, shampoo and even a bottle of some type of perfume.

"Wow," I said. "They went to so much trouble for us."

"They love you," he said. "Almost as much as I do."

"Why would they love me?" I asked. All I had done was leave them.

"Sarah," David added," You need to stop dwelling on leaving, and focus on being. You are someone of value to them and to me. You protected Jack, you physically saved Ruth, and you saved me emotionally. The other kids look to you as a mother figure, and Naomi and her crew look to you as their leader. But right now," he said, "how about you just be my wife?"

"I'd like that," I replied.

"May I carry you to your bath?" he asked.

Normally, I would have felt completely embarrassed by such a gesture, but David had delivered Hope after all. He had seen all of me already, and not at my

209

best, so "Yes," was all I said back. I watched as he walked over to feel the water and decide how he could best deliver me into it.

"I can't believe it," he said, "and I don't know how, but they heated this water."

"Warm water?" I said. I thought perhaps I had already died and gone to Heaven.

David smiled as he walked over and sat down next to me on the rose petal-covered bed. He pulled off my knitted hat and gently ran his fingers through my long brown hair, smoothing it around my face. Next he unzipped my black hoodie and lifted it off of my shoulders and placed it on the floor. I helped him by raising my arms as he lifted my sweater over my head, exposing my full breasts. He took the fingers of his right hand and gently traced them between my breasts and followed the path down my middle.

"Is it okay that I touch you like this?" he asked.

"Yes," I said. Then I reached over and helped him remove his coat. Next he raised his hands as I lifted off his sweater and undershirts. I looked at his exposed chest. It was strong yet lean, and his abdomen revealed the ripples of strength and fitness. I reached out and lightly ran my fingers over his bare skin. I felt his body quiver under my touch.

"Was it like this with Claire?" I asked.

"No," he said. "This is like the first time. This *is* the first time," he added.

He pulled off my ugly black sweat pants and then lifted me from the bed. He walked me over to the waiting tub of what I would soon discover was lukewarm, perfume scented water, and carefully placed me inside. I came alive inside of its cleansing powers and reveled in the scent of times once taken for granted: the smell of the perfume, the feeling of warmth, the strange silence when all of you is emerged in the depths of still waters. I lifted my head out of the stillness and found David standing there, just enjoying my moment of renewal.

"May I wash your hair?" he asked while lathering his hands with the shampoo the others had found. I leaned back in taciturn acceptance as he gently placed his hands in my hair and washed away the past months of struggle. His strong hands massaged my scalp and ran through the lengths of my hair, coating it with the lavender-scented shampoo and the gentle touch of his fingers. He then washed my arms, my shoulders, and my chest. Each inch of my body tingled with delight at his touch. When I could take it no more, I escaped from him by lowering myself deeply into the tub, rinsing my hair and my body. I grabbed the toothpaste and cleaned my mouth before washing my face with the perfumed soap. Feeling completely scented and free from the filth of our past, I reached out for our future. Understanding my gesture, David lifted me from the tub and lay me down on the bed. He wrapped one towel around my body to keep me warm and protected, and used the other one to gently dry my hair. I could never have imagined a more romantic moment, and my heart swelled with love for him. And for what would come to be the last time in a long while, words presented themselves to me, "Love bears all things, believes all things, hopes all things, endures all things." But those things didn't matter now. All that mattered was him and me and this moment in time.

"Your turn," I told him as I slowly sat myself up on the bed and placed my hands on the tops of his shoulders. He easily conceded as I lowered my touch, running my fingers down the small path of his lower abdomen, releasing the top button of his jeans, gently pulling down on the zipper, and at last releasing all of him. I watched as he stood and pulled them down off of his slim hips and long legs. I quivered as for the first time I saw a man as a woman should. He belonged to me, all of him, and it didn't feel dirty or scandalous; it felt pure and right, and incredibly exciting. I watched as he walked over to the tub and lowered himself into the water. He lathered his long hair and body as he prepared himself to meet me. Unable to control myself, I carefully stood and walked the few steps over to the tub. I placed both of my hands in the depths of his long hair and massaged the soapy mix. He moaned with pleasure as he leaned back into my touch. I lathered his face, his beard, eyes, lips.

"I love every inch of you," he said. I leaned over and kissed his lips. The kiss deepened and blossomed and eventually brought him out of the tub. He carried me back to our marriage bed. Our clean bodies melted together as we kissed and touched and explored each other for the first time.

"David," I whispered in his ear. "I'm ready, I'm ready for you."

"I'm more than ready for you," he said, "but we can't. It's too soon. You're not healed enough yet."

"Let's just chance it," I said. My desire for him was, at that moment, worth risking another hemorrhage.

"No," he laughed. "I only just got you; I'm not risking losing you. There are other ways," he said. And then he began kissing me along the narrow strip of my shoulders and along the base of my neck. And I reached out and ran my hands along his chest and down the thin hairline of his lower abdomen. He guided my hand, and we spent the next hours loving and exploring and crying out in the finally released passion that had for so long been suppressed. Fulfilled and exhausted, we crawled under the covers and fell asleep nestled in each other's grateful embrace. *So this was love.*

31

Love Lived

I awakened nestled inside of David's cocooned body. Breathing in his scent that I now knew as my own, I stretched and turned to face him. Keeping his eyes closed, he wrapped his arms around me and pulled me close.

"Hello, wife," he said in a hoarse waking voice that I hoped would grow old with me. Then I remembered that we were not living normal lives in a normal world. For a short time, I had forgotten that we were living in the midst of the apocalypse, and that growing old in anything was highly unlikely.

"David," I said to him, "I wish this moment could last forever."

"It will," he replied. "Embrace yourself in its memory, and in all that we will soon face, retreat to it. It will be with each of us forever."

"What do you mean *in all we will soon face?*" I asked. I didn't want any more hardships; I had had more than enough.

"Sarah, we both know that tough times are not behind us. But it's okay, we'll wrestle through them together."

"Sarah," I heard the soft call of Ruth's voice.

"Yes, Ruth," I said, pulling the covers over me. I could hear the approaching cries of our child, our beautiful Hope. In the passion of marriage, I had forgotten that another life depended on my own.

David leaned over and rekindled a candle to illuminate Ruth's path. Trying not to invade our ceremony, she kept her eyes only on me as she brought me my ravenous infant.

"Thanks, Ruth," I said, accepting Hope and lowering her to my overly full breasts. Ruth turned to go when David spoke to her.

"Ruth," he said, "what you did for us, what all of you did; I can never thank you enough for your kindness. You have no idea the gift you shared."

"You're welcome David," she said as she looked up and met his smile. "And it wasn't just me; it was a complete effort from everyone."

"It was the greatest gift you could have given us," he said. "You are all the family that I never knew I needed, and yet the one that I now could not ever imagine being without. Thank you Ruth."

And then with a shift and a dose of reality he added, "Are Naomi and the others here yet?"

"Yes," she said. "They arrived a few hours ago."

"Okay," David said. "We'll get ourselves together and be out shortly. I guess it's time to move on."

"It is," she said. "But no need to rush. Today is a celebration, and tomorrow's destination can wait." I watched as Ruth turned her back toward us and walked out of our wedding suite.

David leaned over and kissed Hope on her forehead and wrapped his arms around us. "I love you both with all of my life," he said. Then I watched him as he rose and pulled on his jeans. I enjoyed one last look at him, looking incredibly sexy with his uncovered chest and his jeans covering only his bottom half. He caught me looking at him and gave me a wink. "Still like me?" he asked.

"Love you," I answered.

He smiled as he pulled on his shirt before walking around to gather my ugly black sweats and hoodie. He laid them on the bed next to me and waited for Hope to finish her breakfast. After Hope fell into a full-bellied slumber, he scooped her up into his arms and nestled her close. I pulled on my pants and top, but kept my hat off to celebrate my long and newly washed hair; it still smelled like lavender, and the smell once again reminded me of my mother.

"Ready?" he asked.

"Ready," I answered. And then placing my arm inside of his for support, we walked out of the golf cart wedding house and into the small crowd of people who were waiting to greet us. The earthquake brightened skies allowed us to see our newly extended family who had formed a path and welcomed us as if we were just leaving the chapel.

I felt such love for these people who had put great time and effort into giving us a wedding ceremony. I was never really adept at accepting public attention, but this time I welcomed their affections. I knew that they were truly happy for us, but also in what we symbolized. David and I were hope in a time of hopelessness, love in a time of

uncertainty, and good in a time of evil. The ceremony
uplifted us all. I smiled as Ruth greeted us. David handed
Hope to her so that he could truly focus on me. He
supported me as I took my first real walk since my last
medical challenge. I allowed myself to lean on his strength.
Jack came by me on my right and hooked his arm into mine.
Britney walked alongside Jack and held his free hand. I
walked past Jared and the Eirmanns, who were clapping
their hands in congratulatory applause. On the left I saw
Naomi and Norah, Sophie, Jacob, Megan and even the silent
male from the car ride clapping for our union. We passed
people we knew and those whom we had not yet met; all
were a part of our celebration. It was a moment of victory in
a time of defeat. And as we reached the end of our
walkway, I looked up and met eyes of steel that I thought
were long left in the past.

"Claire," I whispered.

And then I saw the eyes, cold and calculated, lean
into slits as the arms of their body raised a weapon toward
me. I felt the final whisper of the words, warm on the back
of my neck, "There is no greater love than this, to lay down
one's life for his friend." *No,* I thought. I fought the words. I
couldn't let them happen. *Please God...no!* I begged.

But before I could react, before I could even scream
a warning, I saw a flash and heard a blast. And as if in slow
motion, I watched as David threw himself in front of me.
And then I felt his body, the one I had completely known,
lay heavy and lifeless on mine. I lay still on the ground and
raised my eyes to meet his, now fallen still. I saw Claire
scream in horror at the realization of what she had done.
And then in malice, or maybe it was just in misguided grief,
she again raised her weapon; this time determined not to
miss her target. I closed my eyes ready and willing to meet
my Romeo in death, and again I heard the blast; but I felt

nothing. Where was the pain? I opened my eyes to see Claire lying dead on the ground, blood pooling around her head. And standing next to her, with the smoking gun that had killed Claire and saved me, was the other man who perhaps loved me enough to die for me, or at least kill for me. It was Lance. And then I watched in silence as Eva, Mitch, and Marcus appeared at his right side. They had come back to save me. How had they known?

Once the chaos of the moment had passed, I could hear the muffled cries of confused children and the whispered words of comforting adults. I crawled out from under David's body and poured myself onto his chest. I felt Jack's strong hand on my back as he and the others allowed me space to grieve. I nestled my face in the nook of David's neck where I breathed deeply, taking in his scent as long as it would last. It mixed with my tears, forming a coating on my face that I would take with me always. After some period of time, I don't know how long, I felt his body begin to stiffen, and I knew that he, the part that made him David, was no longer housed in the physical. It was only then that I backed away and lifted my head. Within the eerie light of the ravaged skies, I could see the progress the group had made. How long had I grieved here? Minutes? Hours? Days? Claire's body was gone, and except for my immediate family, Hope, Jack, Ruth, Britney, Jared, and the Eirmanns, who I realized had been kneeling on the ground with me, the rest had gone to prepare for our continued journey. I lowered my eyes back toward David. *What was I to do now? How could I possibly go on?* And then I felt a breeze begin to stir. It lifted the hair from around my face, drying away my tears, and then slightly rippling the edge of David's shirt. I reached down to touch the exposed skin on his side. My hand jumped with a jolt as I felt movement. Not physical movement of course, but like a part of him, something that was eternal, had left his body and entered mine. I felt his breath in my lungs and it gave me life. And then I heard his voice clearly as if he were whispering right into my ear. He said, "Rejoice even in this, knowing that suffering produces endurance, and endurance produces character, and character produces hope."

"But David!" I yelled. "I don't want it!" And then I whispered, "I just want you." There was no reply, but the feeling of him inside of me remained, and I knew that it always would.

The only sound was Hope who was wailing as if she, too, were mourning the death of her father. And in her cries I heard my purpose. I leaned over and kissed David tenderly on his lips, accepting that I would never again know his physical touch. And then slowly I lifted my head away from his depths and into the reality of life without him. My family met my opened eyes with many unspoken sentiments, and then I heard a stranger's voice; strong, bold, and courageous.

"It's time to bury him," it said. I felt its vibration in my throat and realized that the voice had come from me.

"The others prepared a place," Josh said, motioning toward its direction.

Ruth knelt down beside me and handed me the soft, white blanket from our bed, still holding the blush of marriage in its silken rose petals. Together we wrapped David's body in this shroud that once held promise, and then the others joined us and lifted him, carrying David to his eternal place of rest. I could not release any more tears as they had run dry in both supply and acceptance. I knew that he was no longer here. He was somewhere else; I'm not sure where-but somewhere whole, complete, and reunited with the things he had lost while on this earth. *All except for*

218

me and Hope, I thought, *but we would one day join him;
someday we would get there too.*

"We're here," Josh said, breaking me from my
thoughts.

Before me, I saw a newly dug grave, with piles of
fresh earth covering the deadened ground. Before allowing
everyone to place David's body inside, I lifted the shroud
from his face to have one last look.

"My husband!" I cried out. "My love," I whispered.
Hope began to wail at the sound of my voice. I kissed his
lips one last time and then walked away to accept our child
from Ruth's arms, giving Hope life from my own. I then
watched as earth sealed my marriage in its end. Next to me,
Jack tried to stand strong at my side, but I could see the
stains of tears on his cheeks as he mourned his friend and
mentor. To my left, Ruth stood, her hands covering her face.
And so again I allowed myself to feel. I nestled my face into
Hope's body, my tears replenished as I wept for the man
whom I had both loved and lost; a love too precious for this
hollow land. And as my mourning progressed, I felt dozens
of warm hands of support touching my shoulders. My post-
apocalyptic family and I huddled together in our shared
grief over not just David, but of the loss of the hope our
relationship gave, the reminder of those we had lost before:
Rick, Katie, Jenna; and ultimately over the dire
circumstances in which we would probably lose many
others from our group.

I noticed that in the midst of mourning hope, my
Hope had somehow peacefully quieted. I looked into her
tiny face. And even in infancy, I could see her strength. She
was going to make it. I had to keep going so that she would
make it. In our shared touch, each in our small group reaped
the fertile grounds of Hope, breaking away and knowingly
moving on to the place where just hours ago, David and I

had first arrived in the car. As we approached, I saw Lance and his group, and Norah and hers, sitting in small clusters, silent and waiting. They were waiting for me. I handed a now sleeping Hope to Ruth and grabbed the hand of Jack who had been at my side since David fell, or as I realized, had always been, even when I had left him. I watched as everyone's faces turned toward mine. David had sacrificed himself for me, searching for and finding me, ensuring that I joined him in our pursuit of The Mountain. I was not going to fail him now. Not ever.

I felt Jack's hand as it squeezed mine, his warmth spreading up my arm and into my chest. I turned slightly and looked at him. He nodded. It was time for me to act. It was time for me to speak. It was time for me to accept the role I had been given. Releasing Jack's hand, I straightened my crestfallen shoulders, lifted my head, and stood with the strength of purpose. I thought about David's last words to me – the ones he whispered to me after his death. In some strange way, I suddenly understood Norah's story of the man Job and how he overcame the evil one. And I believed that the things, both good and bad, that had happened and were happening, truly had to be bigger than I or anyone could ever realize. And so I raised my hands to the heavens and bellowed a mournful song with all of my might, because suddenly I was both grieving and accepting. For everyone had been right all along. I was the one who was going to change everything. And the time was now.

"We're taking 70 west," I said in a strong and clear voice, "to Mt. Elbert in Colorado." I looked at the car, fueled and ready to go, and continued with my instructions. "Fill the trunk with all of our supplies, and the seats with our sick, old and young. It will be a long journey. Not all of us will make it, but by God, each of us will try." Movement sparked as the village of twenty or thirty souls prepared to move with life. I met Lance's nod of approval as he helped Eva, Mitch, and Marcus gather their things. I nodded to Norah as she guided Robert, Caitlin, and others in need into the safety of the running car. Finally, I met the eyes of Naomi who looked at me with acknowledgement that perhaps I finally did know who I was.

My name is Sarah Cain, and I am leading my people out of the desert and into the Promised Land.

J.E.Byrne

Hollow Land

J.E.Byrne

NEXT IN THE DEAD LAND SERIES…

PROMISE LAND

…COMING IN DECEMBER 2015

ABOUT THE AUTHOR

Photo: lindajohnsonphotographs.com

As an undergraduate Journalism student at Shippensburg University of Pennsylvania, J.E. took the advice of one of her professors and changed her major to English, specifically focusing on the art of writing. This decision laid the foundation for a career in technical writing, teaching, and eventually fiction writer.

Jodi began her career as a corporate trainer, writing manuals and training programs for computer companies. After starting a family, she earned her MA from Cornerstone University and followed with teaching High School English and Composition. While reading countless novels during course development, she decided to write a series of her own – The *Dead Land* series – (*Dead Land* released in 2013 and *Hollow Land* released in 2014). The planned trilogy combines Jodi's love of fiction, appreciation for young adults and the many challenges they face, and a passion for the spiritual components in life.

Dead Land and *Hollow Land* follow the life of eighteen year-old Sarah Cain as she struggles to survive the pressures and temptations of high school, relationships, self-discovery…and the end of the world.

The Byrne family currently resides in Pennsylvania where J.E. is working on the final installment of the series: *Promise Land.*

J.E.Byrne

Made in the USA
Middletown, DE
21 July 2019